DOCTOR WHO
THE KROTONS

DOCTOR WHO
THE KROTONS

Based on the BBC television serial by Robert Holmes by arrangement with the British Broadcasting Corporation.

Terrance Dicks

Number 99 in the
Doctor Who Library

A TARGET BOOK
published by
the Paperback Division of
W. H. ALLEN & Co. PLC

A Target Book
Published in 1985
by the Paperback Division of
W. H. Allen & Co. PLC
44 Hill Street, London W1X 8LB

First published in Great Britain by
W. H. Allen & Co. PLC in 1985

Printed and bound in Great Britain by
Anchor Brendon Ltd, Tiptree, Essex

The BBC producer of *The Krotons*
was Peter Bryant,
the director was David Maloney.

ISBN 0 426 2018 9 2

Contents

1

A Candidate for Death

In the gloomy, cavernous underground Hall of Learning, the assembled Gonds were waiting. They stood in ranks before the huge, outward-curving silver wall that formed the far end of the Hall. In the centre of the wall, a ramp led up to a closed sliding door.

There was a hush of expectation in the shadowed Hall. When the ceremony was concluded, one or two privileged students, the brightest and best, would pass through that door, achieving the greatest honour known to the People of the Gonds.

They would become Companions of the Krotons — and they would never be seen again.

Selris, Leader of the Council of the Gonds stood waiting impassively by the message-place in the silver wall, the gleaming breastplate of his office making him stand out from his fellow Gonds in their drab one-piece coveralls. His craggy, weathered face and steel-grey hair showed him to be somewhere in his mid-fifties. Yet for all his years, Selris stood as hard and massive as one of the rock pillars that supported the roof of the Hall. A mild man until roused to anger, he was still perfectly prepared to defend his authority with the stone fighting-axe that every adult male Gond wore at his belt.

The little round door of the message-place opened, silently and mysteriously like a metal eye. Selris reached inside and removed the message-sheet and the round door closed.

Selris opened the scroll and studied it for a moment. Then his deep voice boomed out into the tense silence. 'Class three one nine six of the First Grade. The names of the two selected candidates are . . . Male: Abugond.'

A murmur arose from the crowd. Abu, a slender, serious faced young man looked down, modestly accepting the congratulations of his friends.

The low murmurings died away, as Selris spoke again. 'The second name is . . . Female: Vanagond.'

All eyes turned to Vana, a slender fair-haired young girl. Somehow, her outstanding beauty made it hard to believe that she was among the most gifted of her generation of students.

Vana looked delighted, astonished, and a little apprehensive all at the same time. But Thara, the tall, handsome young man standing beside her looked both horrified and afraid. 'No!' he murmured. 'No!'

Selris spoke again. 'Abugond and Vanagond, alone of your fellows you have been chosen to receive the highest honour that can befall a Gond. Soon, you will be Companions of the Krotons. If you will now step forward, you will be invested in your robes of honour.'

Selris turned to a dark, smooth-featured man at his side. 'Eelek . . . '

Eelek stepped forward, a silver cloak over his arm. He nodded towards Abu, who came out of the ranks of the Gonds and stood before him. With ceremonious care Eelek draped the silver cloak about Abu's shoulders. He took a crescent-shaped silver pendant and hung it about Abu's neck . . .

While this was going on, Thara and Vana were

8

arguing in low voices. It would be Vana's turn next for the investiture. She attempted to move away, but Thara was gripping her wrist.

She struggled to free herself. 'Please, Thara!'

'You can't go!' whispered Thara fiercely. 'I won't let you.'

'I must.'

'Look, Vana — we can run away. There's still time . . .'

'You know that's not possible. We must obey the Krotons.'

'Why?' demanded Thara fiercely. 'Why must we obey?'

A big hand clamped down on Thara's shoulder and his father's voice said, 'Because that is the Law of the Krotons.'

They turned. Selris was looming over them. Thara was about to speak, but Selris shook his head sternly, indicating the silver wall. There by the ramp Abu stood waiting, draped in the silver robe with the pendant about his neck.

The door slid silently upwards. Slowly Abu climbed the ramp, and went through the door into the darkness beyond. The door came down behind him.

Behind the City of the Gonds there stretched an area known as the Wasteland, a dead poisoned landscape of rocks and gravel, its monotony broken by the occasional withered plant or petrified tree. Evil-smelling vapours drifted across the bleak terrain.

Since nothing lived there, the area was usually silent, except for the melancholy sighing of the chill wind that haunted the Wastelands.

Suddenly that silence was broken by a strange, wheezing, groaning sound. The square blue shape of a London Police Box materialised at the foot of a steep, rocky cliff.

The door opened and a man emerged. He was on the small side, with a thatch of untidy black hair and a gentle, rather humorous face. He wore baggy checked trousers, a vaguely disreputable-looking frock coat, a wide collared shirt and a scruffy bow tie.

All in all, he was an odd, rather clownish figure. But the little man, like the Police Box behind him, was considerably more impressive than he seemed to be. He was, in fact that wandering Time Lord known only as the Doctor, now in his second incarnation. The Police Box was the TARDIS, an extremely sophisticated space/time craft. Unfortunately, the behaviour of the TARDIS, like that of the Doctor himself, was often erratic in the extreme. Consequently, the Doctor frequently had very little idea as to where, or indeed when he was.

It was this matter that was preoccupying the Doctor's two companions as they followed him from the TARDIS. The first was a brawny youth in Highland dress, complete with kilt, who stood staring around him with his usual air of truculent disapproval.

James Robert McCrimmon, Jamie for short, was a young Scottish piper who had joined the Doctor during the Time Lord's visit to Earth at the time of the Jacobite Rebellion of 1746.

Jamie had been the Doctor's companion through many adventures, and could never make up his mind whether the Doctor was a magician, a madman, or something between the two. One thing Jamie was quite sure of was that the Doctor wasn't safe out on his own and needed someone sensible, such as Jamie himself, to keep him out of trouble.

The Doctor's second companion was also from Earth, though from a time many hundred years after the eighteenth century. A very small, very neat, very precise girl with short dark hair, Zoe Herriot had been a computer operator on a space station before stowing away on board the TARDIS. She wore the simple, functional clothes of her time, a short skirt, blouse, waistcoat and high boots, all in gleaming plasti-cloth.

Like Jamie, she was never quite sure what to make of the Doctor. Zoe was so intelligent and so highly trained that she was a sort of human computer in herself, and she consequently found the Doctor's erratic scatter-brained approach to life and its problems disconcerting in the extreme.

When the companions emerged from the TARDIS all three reacted in their own different ways. Gazing interestedly around him, the Doctor stretched and said happily, 'Lovely, lovely, lovely!', bestowing upon the bleak and hostile landscape the benign approval he accorded to almost everything in the cosmos.

Jamie glared about suspiciously, alert for enemies, and sniffed the drifting vapours. 'Bad eggs! Let's try somewhere else.'

Zoe looked thoughtfully about her, trying to gather evidence for some kind of rational decision. 'Just a minute, Jamie. Where *are* we, Doctor?'

'Och, you don't expect *him* to know, do you?'

'Let's explore, shall we?' said the Doctor happily, ignoring, as usual, the doubts of his companions. 'Just a moment.' He popped back inside the TARDIS and emerged carrying a rolled black object.

Jamie looked at it incredulously. 'Your umbrella?'

The Doctor closed the TARDIS door, opened the umbrella — and pointed skywards. 'Twin suns. Bound to be hot.'

Zoe looked up. Two fiery balls hung in the sky, doing their best to glow through the overcast clouds. The Doctor was right, thought Zoe. The climate was

11

both dull and oppressive at the same time. The twin suns settled one thing — they weren't on Earth.

The Doctor set off apparently at random across the barren landscape. Resignedly, Jamie and Zoe followed.

'I don't think I like it here much,' said Zoe. 'It looks — dead.'

'Aye, and it smells dead too.'

'Sulphur, isn't it?' Zoe looked at the Doctor. 'Could be poisonous.'

'Nonsense. The TARDIS instruments would have warned us. It's just a mixture of ozone and sulphur. Very bracing.'

They trudged across the featureless landscape for some time. Looking round, Zoe saw that they were in a kind of enormous crater. The ground began to slope gently upwards as they neared the low rise that formed the crater's edge. Suddenly the Doctor stopped and picked up a gleaming shard from the ground at his feet.

'What's that?' asked Jamie.

'A most interesting mineral formation. Magnesium silicate.'

'He means mica,' explained Zoe.

Jamie grunted, none the wiser.

The Doctor scrambled to the top of the rise, and waved his umbrella triumphantly. 'Aha! All dead, is it?'

Zoe came to join him. Beyond the rise the ground sloped sharply downwards again into a kind of natural hollow. Inside the hollow, and filling it almost completely there was a city.

Perhaps city was too grand a word, thought Zoe as she studied it. It looked more like a village, a settlement or a colony. It consisted of a cluster of low stone buildings on either side of a broad shallow river,

12

the banks of which were lined with luxurious vegetation. The largest building of all seemed to be built into the ridge on which they stood.

'Yes, fascinating architecture,' said the Doctor. 'It's more typical of a low-gravity planet, but as far as I can tell this is fairly close to Earth-normal.' He jumped up and down experimentally.

Zoe studied the city thoughtfully. 'An Inca-type culture, perhaps. That big building below could be a temple.'

'Yes, very possibly . . . '

They were interrupted by a shout from behind them. 'Hey, Doctor, down here. Come and see!'

The Doctor turned. 'Let's see what Jamie's found. Careful, Zoe.' Taking Zoe's arm, he helped her to scramble back down the slope.

They found Jamie a little below them and some way to their right, standing in front of a huge dully gleaming section that seemed to bulge out of the side of the ridge.

'What is it, Jamie?' asked Zoe.

Jamie shrugged. 'I dunno. Look, there's a kind of ramp.'

And indeed, before the gleaming section, the ground sloped upwards with unnatural smoothness.

'There's a door too,' said Zoe.

Set into the centre of the area was an oddly shaped door, a kind of diamond shape with the upper and lower points cut off by horizontal lines.

Studying its position, Zoe realised that it could well be some kind of back door to the temple-like building on the other side of the ridge. Though if that was the case and the building stretched clear *through* the ridge it must be enormous . . .

'Do you think it's some kind of wall, Doctor? Because if it is —'

'No, I hardly think so, Zoe. Not a wall, exactly.'

The Doctor walked up the ramp and peered at the dully gleaming surface.

Jamie sniffed, 'That bad egg smell's a lot stronger here.'

The Doctor was busily scratching at the surface with the ferrule of his umbrella and muttering to himself. 'Hmm, how very fascinating.'

Zoe followed him up the ramp and Jamie came to join them. 'This bit here — it's metal, isn't it?'

Zoe nodded. 'Covered in moss and lichen, though.' Which meant, thought Zoe, that it had been here for a very long time.

The Doctor was holding the flat of his palm against the dully, gleaming surface. 'Metal? Would you say so?' All at once he leaped back. 'I think we'd better go.'

By now Zoe's scientific curiousity was aroused. 'But why, Doctor?'

'Because this isn't a wall or a building. It's a machine!'

The door began gliding smoothly upwards. The Doctor grabbed his two companions and almost dragged them behind the shelter of a nearby boulder. They watched fascinated from their hiding place as the door slid fully open.

After a moment a young man emerged. He wore a silver cloak and a pendant, and his face was utterly, terrifyingly blank. He stood there for a moment staring vacantly, as the door came down behind him.

Jamie stared hard at the young man, puzzled by his odd manner. 'What's the matter with him?'

The Doctor too, was watching intently. 'Sssh!'

Circular hatches slid open in the wall on either side of the door and twin nozzles appeared. The Doctor was about to shout a warning, but already it was too late.

Vapour hissed fiercely from the nozzles, forming a thick cloud engulfing the young man completely. There came one terrible scream — then silence.

The cloud dispersed, drifting away.

The silver-cloaked young man had disappeared and all that was left of him was the pendant that had hung around his neck.

The Doctor and his companions emerged from their hiding place. Everything was silent.

Before the Doctor could stop him, Jamie ran up the ramp and picked up the pendant. It crumbled to nothingness in his hands.

'Poor man,' said Zoe softly. There was nothing left of him, she thought. Nothing at all.

Jamie said wonderingly, 'What happened to him, Doctor? What is that thing?'

'I'm not sure,' said the Doctor grimly. 'But whatever it is, I think we'll do well to keep away from it.'

He led the way back up the ridge.

'Where are we going?' called Zoe.

'To that temple place. We shall try approaching this problem from the other side!'

In the Hall of Learning, Eelek was helping Vana into her robe. He hung the silver pendant about ner neck.

She moved forward, and stood waiting before the door.

2

The Rescue

As Vana stood by the door, waiting, like Abu and so
many others before, to become a Companion of the
Krotons, Thara was arguing furiously with his father
Selris.

'Father, please, give the order that she doesn't have
to go. You're our leader.'

Selris looked not unsympathetically at his son. Tall
and strong, jaw jutting determinedly, Thara was, in so
many ways, a younger version of himself. But Selris's
duty was quite clear. 'The Krotons have chosen Vana.
It is a great honour.' And that, Selris's manner
implied, was that. The matter was closed.

'The Krotons!' snarled Thara. 'Why do we obey
their orders? We don't even know if they exist!'

He sprang forward, placing himself between Vana
and the door.

Vana was shocked by such blasphemy. 'Thara! You
mustn't say things like that!'

Eelek tried to push Thara aside. 'Get out of the
way!'

But Thara was taller and stronger than Eelek. He
refused to budge. 'She is not going into that machine!'

'She has to,' said Eelek flatly. 'No-one defies the
Krotons.' Once again he tried to thrust Thara aside.

'All right!' said Thara grimly. Grabbing Vana's arm he swung her behind him, then drew the axe from his belt, glaring defiantly at Eelek. 'Come on, then!'

But Eelek was a politician, not a fighter. 'Don't be stupid,' he said wearily, and beckoned to the Learning Hall Guards.

'Stop, Thara!' shouted Selris, fearful that his son would be injured, perhaps even killed.

Eelek turned to the approaching guards. 'Disarm him!'

Thara brandished his axe. 'Keep back!'

The guards hesitated. Like his father, Thara was a skilled and powerful fighter. They would overcome him in time but some of them would die doing it.

At this precise moment, the Doctor, Jamie and Zoe appeared at the top of the broad stone steps leading down into the underground hall.

They had found the city itself deserted, naturally enough since most of the Gonds were packed into the Hall of Learning for the ceremony. The temple too had appeared to be deserted. Attracted by the sound of voices they had made their way to the steps that led down into the Hall of Learning. Only now did they find themselves discovered and opposed, as astonished guards moved in to surround them. The guards were armed with long savage-looking pikes with gleaming diamond shaped blades at the tip.

'What if they're not friendly?' asked Zoe worriedly.

'Just let me talk to them.' The Doctor stepped forward with a friendly smile. The guards raised their pikes and the Doctor stepped back hurriedly. 'We are friends!' The guards didn't seem impressed. 'Don't be afraid,' he said encouragingly. 'We're not going to hurt you.' Still no response.

'I think we're in for trouble, Doctor,' warned Jamie

18

cheerfully. He seemed to be looking forward to it.

At last one of the guards, a brown fierce-looking fellow and obviously some kind of leader, stepped forward and said, 'Who are you?'

'Never mind that,' said the Doctor impatiently. 'Tell your men to let us pass.'

'Answer me. Who are you and where are you from?'

The Doctor sighed. 'We haven't time for explanations now.'

'You're not Gonds,' said the guard captain accusingly, as if this in itself was a crime. 'Your clothes, the way you're dressed . . . '

'Look,' said the Doctor, 'I assure you that we're friendly.'

Jamie squared up to the guard captain. 'Are you going to let us by or not?'

Zoe meanwhile had been watching events at the far end of the crowded hall. 'Doctor, look!' she called.

At the other end of the hall another group of guards was closing in on Thara, who was standing protectively in front of Vana.

Thara glared at the nearest guard, his axe raised to strike. 'I'm warning you, one step nearer . . . '

Eelek turned to Selris. 'He's your son. Do something about him.'

'Eelek's enjoying this,' thought Selris bitterly. He had long been a rival for the leadership. He would do anything that could bring Selris and his family into disrepute.

'Thara, be reasonable,' shouted Selris. 'The Krotons have sent for Vana.'

'She's not going. Nobody ever comes back from there . . . ' Thara broke off. The slight distraction had enabled one of the guards to sidle closer. Suddenly the razor-sharp edge of a pike-blade was inches from Thara's throat.

He could dodge and kill this one pikeman, thought Thara, but the others . . .

He felt Vana struggling to pull free. 'Let me go, Thara,' she pleaded. 'I don't want them to hurt you.'

Realising that unless he surrendered he would be probably cut down before Vana's eyes, Thara released her and stepped back, returning the axe to his belt.

The Doctor and his companions were watching all this from the steps. 'What's happening to that girl?' asked Zoe.

Jamie said, 'She's wearing robes just like that man who we saw killed!'

Zoe turned to the Doctor in horror. 'Is she going to be sacrificed?'

'Oh, I hardly think so, Zoe. These people are too civilised for that.'

'Whatever it is, we ought to stop it,' muttered Jamie.

The Doctor raised his voice commandingly. 'Wait!' he called. 'Wait a minute.'

Scandalised, the guard captain ordered, 'Do not interrupt the ceremony!' He turned to his men. 'Take them!'

Jamie glared at him. 'You wouldn't talk so brave without your guards behind you. Why don't you have a go?'

The guard captain held up his hand to halt his men. 'Wait — get back!' He swung round on Jamie. 'I am Axus! I accept your challenge!'

'That's just fine with me,' said Jamie happily.

'Now, Jamie,' said the Doctor reprovingly, 'there's no need to be rash.'

'Don't worry, Doctor. I'll soon deal with this laddie.'

At a sign from Axus, one of the guards offered Jamie his axe. Scornfully, Jamie waved it away. 'I'll no' be needing that.' If he couldn't have his trusty claymore he preferred to trust his bare hands rather than risk using an unfamiliar weapon.

Arms outstretched like something between a boxer and a wrestler, Jamie squared up to his opponent. Axus lashed out with his axe. Quickly, Jamie ducked and stepped back.

'Look out Jamie!' called Zoe.

Axus sprang forward, his arm raised to strike, and Jamie stepped inside the upraised arm and grabbed Axus's wrist, holding the axe-arm high.

The two fighters were locked motionless for a moment, their strength almost perfectly matched. Then, slowly, very slowly, Jamie began forcing the captain's axe-arm downwards. With a final heave and thrust, Jamie wrenched the axe from Axus's hand and gave him a shove that sent him flying to the ground.

Seeing that the fight was over, and Jamie unhurt, Zoe looked back across the hall. 'Doctor, look!' she called. 'The girl . . . '

The door in the silver wall was sliding upwards. Vana gave Thara one last agonised look and then walked slowly up the ramp and disappeared into darkness. The door slid down behind her.

Pushing past the confused and distracted guards, the Doctor and his friends made their way to the other side of the Hall.

Eelek stared haughtily at them. 'Who are these people? What is going on?'

'The very question I was going to ask,' said the Doctor indignantly. 'What is happening here?'

The guard captain picked himself up, recovered his axe and came hurrying across the hall.

'They forced their way in here, Eelek.'

Selris was looking at the strangers in amazement. 'Who are you? Where do you come from?'

'Oh, I'll explain that later,' said the Doctor hurriedly.

Jamie said, 'Believe me, you wouldn't understand if we told you.'

'We come from another planet, another world,' said Zoe — and realised immediately from her listeners' reaction that Jamie had been right.

'That girl,' said the Doctor, 'Would you mind telling us where she's gone?'

'How can you be from another planet?' growled Selris.

Jamie said truculently, 'Look, we're wasting time! Where's that girl gone, that's what we want to know.'

'And what's behind that wall?' asked Zoe.

'They've sent her to join the Krotons,' said Thara despairingly.

Zoe stared at him. 'What are the Krotons?'

'You really don't know?' asked Selris.

Thara said impatiently, 'How could they — if they really are from another planet.' He turned to Zoe. 'The Krotons live in that machine — so we are told.'

Selris said patiently. 'Vana is joining the Krotons. It's a great honour for a Gond to become a Companion of the Krotons.'

'Honour!' said Thara scornfully. 'She didn't really want to go. No one ever wants to disappear into that thing.'

Eelek looked disparagingly at these oddly dressed newcomers. 'Who are you? Why are you asking all these questions?'

'Because,' said the Doctor, 'just a few minutes ago we saw a young man wearing a silver cloak like that girl — Vana, is it? Anyway, we saw him killed.'

'Abugond,' whispered Thara. 'It must have been Abugond.'

'Ridiculous,' sneered Eelek. 'How can these

strangers have seen Abugond?'

'Abugond is with the Krotons,' said Selris solemnly.

'Well, we saw *somebody* killed,' said Jamie bluntly. 'He left the machine and he was —' Jamie hesitated, at a loss to find words to describe what had happened.

'He was vaporised,' said Zoe.

Jamie nodded. 'Aye, that's right. Outside a door just like this one, only round at the other side of this thing.' He pointed. 'Out there!'

'You have been in the Wasteland?' whispered Selris.

'You are contaminated,' said Eelek. 'Nobody ever goes in the Wasteland.' He raised his voice. 'Stand back. They are contaminated.'

The effect was sudden and dramatic. The encircling Gonds stepped hurriedly back, and the Doctor and his friends found themselves isolated.

'Why does no-one go into the Wasteland?' asked Zoe.

'It is poisoned. Soon you will die.'

'Nonsense!' said the Doctor. 'It may have been poisoned at one time, but I assure you it's quite safe now.'

Jamie tugged at his sleeve. 'Doctor, that girl. If she comes out the other side in the same way . . . '

The Doctor nodded vigorously. 'Quite right, Jamie. We must try to save her. Come on.'

He hurried towards the steps and the others followed. No-one made any attempts to stop them, presumably through the fear of contamination.

Selris called after them, 'Where are you going?'

Zoe's voice came back. 'To the Wasteland.'

'But you can't. It is against the law of the Krotons!'

By now the Doctor and his friends were out of sight.

'I'm going with them,' said Thara suddenly, and hurried towards the stairs.

'Thara come back!' shouted Selris.

'If they can go to the Wasteland, so can I!'

'Come back, my son,' called Selris in anguish. 'You too will die!'

The Doctor, Jamie and Zoe slithered down the rocks and came panting to a halt outside the oddly-shaped door set into the ridge in the Wasteland.

'Well, there it is,' said Jamie grimly.

The Doctor nodded. 'Yes . . . I wonder how long we've got. I imagine there isn't much time.'

He strode up the ramp.

'What are you going to do, Doctor?' called Zoe.

'You two stay back there, out of the way . . . '

They heard a pounding of footsteps and the young man they'd seen protesting in the underground Hall came running to join them. 'Please, can I help you?'

The Doctor said, 'Not really I'm afraid, Mr er . . . ?'

'I am Thara.'

The Doctor was looking about him. 'Bring me a handful of loose stones, would you?'

Thara gave him an astonished look. 'What? What for?'

'You want to help, don't you?' snapped the Doctor.

'Yes . . . yes, of course.' Thara hurried to a bank of loose stones and came running back with a handful of small rocks and pebbles.

The Doctor selected two smallish, round ones and jammed them into the sockets from which the acid vapour had emerged. 'Right! Now, get out of the way all of you. Over there somewhere, behind those boulders.'

'Be careful, Doctor,' said Zoe. 'I think I can hear something. A kind of humming, a vibration.'

'I know, Zoe, so can I. I'm nearer than you, remember!'

24

The door slid slowly open and Vana stumbled out onto the ramp.

There was little resemblance to the attractive, intelligent girl they had glimpsed in the underground Hall. Her steps were shambling, her face empty and vacant. Thara stared at her in horror. 'Vana! What have they done to you?'

He jumped to his feet, but Jamie grabbed him and pulled him into cover. 'Keep down!'

As soon as Vana was clear of the doorway, the Doctor darted forward, grabbed her around the waist and began hustling her down the ramp. Already a muffled, hissing was coming from the blocked jets.

'Quickly, Doctor,' shouted Zoe. The hissing sound grew louder and the jamming rocks began to vibrate.

'Doctor, look out!' shouted Jamie. He jumped to his feet and ran forward. The pressure build-up forced the looser of the two rocks from its place. Corrosive vapour poured from the unblocked jet.

The Doctor moved with astonishing speed. With one hand he thrust Vana forward off the ramp and in the same moment, touched the spring that opened his umbrella, swinging it over his shoulder so that it acted as a shield.

Jamie grabbed Vana and pulled her clear. Seconds later, the Doctor too was safely out of range. The hissing of the jet stopped, as the corrosive spray died away.

Jamie lowered Vana gently to the ground and Thara knelt beside her. 'Vana? Vana, what's wrong?'

She opened her eyes and stared at him, with no sign of recognition.

'What's happened?' whispered Thara. 'What have they done to her?'

The Doctor was gazing indignantly at the tattered remains of his umbrella. The corrosive vapour had

25

reduced it to a skeleton of warped metal struts and tattered silk. 'Vandals! Just look at that!'

'That could have been you, Doctor,' pointed out Zoe.

'My favourite umbrella!' The Doctor sadly tossed the twisted remains away.

Thara was almost frantic with worry. 'She doesn't know me, Doctor. She doesn't speak or anything.'

Jamie glared at the door. 'It must be something your Krotons have done to her.'

The Doctor was still testing Vana's reflexes. 'Hmm . . . almost catatonic! Dear me . . . '

'Isn't there anything you can do?' asked Zoe worriedly.

'I am not a doctor of medicine,' snapped the Doctor — a little unfairly, since he was in fact a doctor of almost everything. 'However, as long as there's no tissue damage . . . She needs rest and quiet. Is there somewhere we can take her, Thara?'

'My father Selris's house is quite near — on the edge of the community.'

'Good. We'll take her there, then. Give her a hand, will you?'

Thara helped Vana to her feet. Half-supporting, half-carrying, he led her away.

Slowly the little party made its way across the Wasteland. As they moved Zoe gave one last glance over her shoulder at the mysterious door.

What happened inside there? What evil force turned bright, intelligent young people into stumbling mindless idiots, and then did its best to destroy them utterly?

What kind of monsters were hiding behind that door?

3

The Rebels

Zoe swigged gratefully at the liquid in the earthen-
ware mug. She wasn't quite sure what she was
drinking — it was fiery and fruity at the same time.
But together with the simple meal of cheese and fruit
provided by Selris, it had refreshed and revived her
after their ordeal in the Wastelands and the journey
back. Even Jamie had admitted that whatever the
drink was, it was, 'No' bad at all!'

Selris, newly returned from the Hall of Learning,
had been shocked by their story, and horrified by
Vana's condition. Even now he could scarcely take it
in. 'It's almost impossible to believe. The Krotons
have always been our friends — our benefactors.'

Zoe said, 'Well, you've only got to look at what
they've done to Vana.'

Selris nodded, looking across to the curtained
alcove on the far side of the simply furnished room,
where the Doctor was attending to Vana.

At that moment the curtain was drawn back and
Thara emerged. Jamie looked up, 'How is she?'

'Just the same.' Grim faced, Thara strode out of the
room without another word. Zoe looked worriedly
after him, wondering where he was going and what he
planned to do.

Jamie rose and looked inside the alcove where Vana lay stretched out on the bed, her eyes open and staring blankly at the ceiling.

The Doctor was leaning over her, in his shirt-sleeves, dangling his old-fashioned pocket watch on its gold chain in front of her eyes. The watch swung gently to and fro and Vana was following it with her eyes.

The Doctor was speaking in a low, soothing voice. 'Now you are resting . . . softly resting . . . your mind is empty . . . You are resting. You feel sleepy . . . so sleepy, Vana . . . very sleepy . . . '

Jamie looked on in astonishment. Suddenly he found his own eyelids heavy and his head beginning to nod. Hurriedly he turned away. Some more of the Doctor's magic, he thought. Perhaps he was saying a spell. He went back to join Zoe and Selris on the other side of the big room.

Selris was explaining things to Zoe. ' . . . and so, at the appointed times our best students enter the machine to join the Krotons. They can't all have been murdered, surely?'

'It's just possible, you know. If they had, you wouldn't know because that poison spray just . . . '

She shuddered at the memory.

'It dissolves everything,' said Jamie bluntly. 'And in any case, you people never go into the Wasteland.'

'But why have they done it? Why kill our best students?' asked Selris helplessly.

Zoe looked round the room. It was plainly and simply furnished with the basics of civilised living. There were chairs, tables, a bed, couches to sit on, scattered rugs on the floor. Basic comforts, but no really advanced technology. Perhaps the Krotons planned to limit the development of Gond civilisation by creaming off the best brains . . . 'What are they

28

like, these Krotons?'

'No living person has ever seen them. They never come out of the machine.'

'Never?'

'Not for thousands of years. Not since the beginning'

Before Zoe could ask any more questions the Doctor came out of the alcove, shrugging into his coat.

Zoe looked up. 'How is she?'

'Asleep at last.'

'Will she be all right?'

'I hope so. It's difficult to say.'

'She was one of our most brilliant students,' said Selris sadly.

'The Doctor raised his eyebrows. 'Really? Competiton for you, Zoe!'

Zoe gave him a quelling look. 'Apparently no-one's ever seen these Krotons, Doctor.'

Jamie said, 'Aye, that's right. They never come out of that machine.'

They both looked expectantly at the Doctor as if expecting him to come up with a solution to the mystery on the spot. The Doctor however decided he needed more information. 'How did all this begin, Selris?'

'According to our legends, great silver men came out of the sky and built a house among us. The Gonds attacked them and the silver men caused a poisonous rain to fall, killing hundreds of our people and turning the ground black.'

Jamie grunted. 'That accounts for yon Wasteland.'

Selris nodded. 'Yes, that is so. It was afterwards said that anyone who set foot there died in terrible pain . . . '

In the Hall of Learning, the Custodian moved

29

reverently amongst the dark shapes of the Teaching Machines.

The Machines stood in long rows, half-concealed behind the pillars to one side of the stairs. The area was gloomy and shadowed, and the Custodian lit his way with a magic staff that was a gift of the Krotons. You touched a stud at one end and light appeared at the other. It was the badge of the Custodian's office and he carried it with immense pride.

He was a slight, balding man with a beaky nose and a bushy moustache. Not in fact a very imposing guardian, though this mattered little since his duties were purely nominal.

The Teaching Machines maintained themselves, and as for guarding them — well, who would dare to attack the Hall of Learning, the very centre of Kroton authority?

Absorbed in the routine of his task, the Custodian failed to notice shadowy figures flitting between the pillars in the darkened hall.

He checked the last Teaching Machine, turned away — and suddenly strong hands caught him and threw him to the ground. Someone snatched the torch from his hands and shone it on his face.

The Custodian struggled feebly, but he was held too strongly to move. He became aware of a handful of shapes looming over him.

'Who are you?' he quavered. 'What are you doing here? It is forbidden to enter the Learning Hall at this time. The Law of the Krotons clearly states . . . '

One of the dark shapes leaned forward menacingly. 'Ah, yes! The Krotons. You must know a lot about them?'

'What do you mean?'

'You're their servant aren't you?' accused another voice. 'You work for them.'

'I am only the Custodian of the Hall of Learning.'

The first voice said mockingly. 'Yes, of course. Then you can tell us all we want to know.'

'I am forbidden to discuss the secrets of the Krotons.'

'We just want to know how to get at them. We want to see these Krotons for ourselves.'

The Custodian was horrified. 'But no-one has ever seen the Krotons. Not for thousands of years.'

'You're sure they don't come out of that machine in the darkness when there's no-one here?'

'Come out? The Krotons? Never!'

'Then how do they give their commands? Answer me!'

'There are Messages, left in the appointed place. You must know that.'

'What else?'

'Sometimes there is a voice,' admitted the Custodian reluctantly.

'But you've never seen them? There's no way inside the Machine?'

'Only the Companions of the Krotons may enter.'

'Yes,' said the voice bitterly. 'And now we know what happens to them. But you can summon the Krotons — *can't you?* Answer!'

'It is not for me to summon the Krotons. I obey their commands.'

There was a moment of silence, then the Custodian heard his captors muttering amongst themselves.

The first voice said angrily. 'If we can't get inside the Machine, then we must fetch the Krotons out!'

'How can we do that?'

'By smashing their precious Teaching Machines.'

'Smash the Machines?' gasped the Custodian. 'You can't! The Krotons will destroy us all!'

He made a desperate attempt to escape, and

actually succeeded in breaking free for a moment, before the many hands of his attackers pulled him down again.

'Here, tie his hands,' ordered the leader. 'Careful, I don't want him hurt. You'd better gag him as well.'

As his arm and legs were bound with lengths of cord, and a piece of rag bound across his mouth, the Custodian realised with horror that the chief of his attackers was Thara, son of Selris, leader of the Council of the Gonds.

'Go on, Selris. What happened after this war with the Krotons?' asked Jamie.

'It was all so long ago. According to our legends, since then we have lived in peace. The Krotons never show themselves, but we learn from them, through the Teaching Machines.'

Zoe's interest was aroused. 'Teaching Machines?'

'They are in the Learning Hall, where you were today. They fill the mind with knowledge.'

The Doctor frowned. 'And does everyone use these Machines?'

'When they are young, yes. That is the Law.'

'Whose law, Selris?' demanded the Doctor.

'Ours. The Council of the Gonds.'

'But weren't your laws also given you by the Teaching Machines — by the Krotons, hmm?'

'Yes, that is true,' said Selris, almost as if realising the fact for the first time. 'Our laws, our science, our culture, everything we have has come from the Teaching Machines.'

'Yes . . . self perpetuating slavery,' muttered the Doctor. 'And at regular intervals, the Krotons choose your most promising students to be their Companions?'

Selris nodded, a look of dawning horror on his face.

'Doctor, do you . . . do you think they have all been killed?'

'Well, we *saw* one killed,' said Jamie bluntly.

Zoe turned to the Doctor. 'Why are the Krotons doing it, Doctor? What's their reason?'

'I don't know — yet. But it's time it was stopped. High time!'

'How shall I tell the people?' asked Selris helplessly. 'How can I explain?'

'Explain what?' exploded Jamie. 'Just tell them the truth.'

'That they've been tricked? That for thousands of years our best students have been murdered by the Krotons.'

'Why?' asked Zoe. 'What are you afraid of?'

'Another war between your people and the Krotons, I should imagine,' said the Doctor.

Selris nodded, the responsibilities of his leadership weighing heavily upon him. 'If I tell them, and if they attack the Krotons, there could be terrible bloodshed, as there was before. Another massacre. Another Wasteland here, instead of our community.'

'Selris!' A young Gond rushed into the room, taller and more slightly built than the rest they'd seen, with a thin, intellectual face.

Selris smiled. 'Ah, Beta, I thought you'd be along to meet our guests.' He turned to the others. 'Beta here is our Controller of Science, and also my son's good friend.'

'That's why I'm here,' gasped Beta. 'Because of Thara. He was at the Hall of Students, talking to the others. He and some of his friends, all the hot-headed ones, have gone out to the Hall of Learning. They're going to attack the Krotons — wreck the Teaching Machines if they have to, to fetch them out of hiding. You've got to stop them, Selris. I came as quickly as I could, but they'll be there by now.'

'Then it's too late.'

The Doctor jumped to his feet. 'Not if we cut across the Wasteland.'

Beta gave him a look of astonished horror. 'The Wasteland? But it's poisonous . . . '

'Nonsense. It may have been once, but any poison wore off long ago.'

'That's right,' said Jamie, pleased at the prospect of a little action. 'We've been through your Wasteland twice today and we're just fine. Come on!'

Talking about attacking the Teaching Machines was easy enough, but actually doing it was quite another. Thara's fellow students had a lifetime of conditioning to overcome and he had to whip up their courage all over again before they were ready to take action.

Axes in their hands, they stood around the bulky shape of the nearest Teaching Machine. All the Machines were exactly the same design — a console, a vision screen, a chair for the student, and a metal helmet suspended over the chair by a flexible arm.

'Well, come on!' shouted Thara at last. Raising his axe high, he brought it smashing down on the console. A crack appeared in the smooth gleaming surface. The others waited aghast, expecting some unimaginable terror — a bolt of lighting, perhaps even an angry Kroton. Nothing happened.

Emboldened, Thara raised his axe and struck again and again. The console began to splinter. With yells of triumph, the others ran to join him. Soon the console was shuddering under a rain of axe-blows.

Bound and gagged at the base of a pillar, the Custodian looked on in unbelieving horror.

The great Kroton Machine, the one built into the

34

Learning Hall, was alive.

Not perhaps in the way that a living, thinking being is alive. But it was so elaborately programmed to serve the interests of its unseen masters, so well-equipped with various means of information-gathering, evaluating, methods of attack and defence, that at times it could react with something very like intelligence.

It was doing so now.

In the control room at the heart of the Machine, instruments clicked and whirred, and spools revolved into life. A monitor screen lit up.

An observation servo-mechanism, in essence no more than a black box with a lens, slid forward on a long extensible rod and peered curiously into the monitor.

The Teaching Machine was a twisted pile of plastic and shattered circuitry. 'That should fetch them out!' yelled Thara.

By now the blood of the little band of rebellious students was up. 'Come on!' screamed one of them, hitherto the most timid. 'Let's wreck another!'

A voice boomed from out of the air. 'STOP!'

It was a loud, booming voice, with a harsh, throaty grating to it. Thara and his little band of rebels froze instantly.

'THIS IS A WARNING. LEAVE THE HALL. ALL GONDS LEAVE THE HALL NOW!'

'The Krotons,' muttered one of the students fearfully.

'LEAVE THE HALL. ALL GONDS LEAVE THE HALL NOW.'

The students began edging away, but Thara had gone too far to be frightened off now. 'That's just a voice,' he shouted. 'Don't be afraid!'

35

'THIS IS A WARNING.'

It was a warning Thara chose to ignore. 'Come out, you Krotons! Come out and fight!' He attacked the next Teaching Machine.

Thara's enthusiasm gave the others new courage. 'Murderers!' shrieked the timid student, now bold again. Together with the others he joined in the attack.

'Thara! Stop!'

Suddenly Selris was there, shoving Thara away from the Teachine Machine. At the same time the Doctor turned to the excited group of students and shooed them away like a flock of hens.

'Listen to me,' he shouted. 'This will do no good. No good at all. These Krotons must have enormous scientific powers. You can't defeat them with axes!'

He snatched the axe from Thara's hand and brandished it reprovingly at him.

The picture on the monitor showed the little group of students arguing amongst themselves. At the centre of the group stood one smaller and dressed differently from the rest. He was waving one of the primitive weapons.

With impeccable machine logic the servo-mechanism decided that this primitive was obviously the leader, inciting the rest to attack. Its data bank told it that when the leader was destroyed primitive attackers would usually flee.

Transferring the Doctor's image to its memory bank, the servo-mechanism moved away to take the necessary action.

Outside in the Learning Hall, the Doctor handed the axe back to Thara. 'Now, if this was an atomic laser it might be more use.'

'Atomic laser?' said Thara doubtfully. 'Is that better than an axe?'

'Look at the damage you've done,' growled Selris. 'Completely senseless.'

Thara was unrepentant. 'Look what they did to our friends!'

'Destroying the machines won't revenge Abu, or help Vana, will it?'

'We can't get in there,' muttered one of the students. 'If we attack their machines . . . '

'The Krotons will come out!' finished Thara.

There was a whirring sound and a round hatch beside the machine door slid open.

'I think *something's* coming out, right now,' said the Doctor worriedly.

And so it was. The 'something' was a gleaming, articulated metal snake, its whole head composed of a single glowing lens. The snake extruded from the hatchway and hovered, swaying in the air like a cobra looking for a victim.

'Doctor, what is it?' whispered Zoe fearfully.

'I don't know, Zoe, but whatever it is, we'd better keep well away from it.'

Suddenly the metal snake seemed to spot the little group and it streaked through the air towards them. They backed hurriedly away as it hovered in front of them, swaying to and fro hypnotically.

'What's it doing?' whispered Thara.

Zoe studied the strange object thoughtfully. 'Doctor, it seems to be *looking* at us.'

'How can it?' asked Jamie nervously. 'It's no' alive — is it?'

The lens transmitted the information back. The face of the primitive leader was the face before the lens. It had found its target. Relentlessly, the metal snake homed in on the Doctor, singling him out from the others.

'Doctor, it's after *you!*' gasped Zoe.

The Doctor backed away still further. Tripping over a chunk of the broken Teaching Machine he fell over backwards . . .

The snake zoomed forwards aiming directly for his face. Helpless, flat on his back, the Doctor threw up his arms in a vain attempt to shield himself . . .

4

The Genius

All at once the metal snake started to waver, as if it had lost its sense of direction. It began weaving to and fro in the air, almost as if it had suddenly gone blind.

Still keeping his face covered, and peeping through his fingers the Doctor started to get up.

'Doctor, don't move,' called Zoe.

The Doctor got carefully to his feet. 'It's all right, Zoe. I'm quite safe!'

Jamie wasn't convinced. 'I wouldna be so sure.'

'Look,' said the Doctor happily.

He took his hands away from his face.

The metal snake, still sweeping to and fro, checked its swing and zoomed straight for the Doctor.

Calmly, the Doctor covered his face with his hands. Confused once more, the metal snake swung vaguely backwards and forwards, resuming its search.

Suddenly Zoe understood. 'Pattern recognition!'

'Exactly, Zoe,' said the Doctor from behind his hands. 'And the pattern is obviously my face!'

Selris stared at him. 'Then you mean that that thing was sent out to attack you — and only you?'

'So it seems. Flattering, isn't it?'

Zoe said slowly. 'Then the Krotons must know who you are — or know what you look like.'

'Yes, so they must, Zoe. Therefore they must have a scanner in the hull of the machine somewhere. If we can find it, we may be able to make contact with them and —'

In his excitement, the Doctor dropped his hands from his face. The metal snake spotted him at once and began zipping towards him. With a yell of alarm, the Doctor threw himself to one side.

The timid student suddenly saw his chance for real glory. As the snake waved about in quest of the Doctor, he leaped forward, swinging with his axe.

The metal snake froze, and hung poised for a moment, staring at him with its single glowing eye. Then a jet of corrosive vapour hissed out from a nozzle set just beneath the lens. The student gave one terrible scream . . .

When the vapour dispersed he had vanished. All that remained was the axe, flung to one side by his dying hand.

'Look, Doctor, it's going back,' shouted Jamie.

The metal snake was retracing, sliding back into the machine. It grew shorter and shorter until the lens went back through the circular opening, and the hatch slid closed.

Once again, the Doctor climbed to his feet. 'Yes . . . I'm afraid that poor fellow must have confused the attack mechanism.'

Jamie stared at him. 'Eh?'

'It was programmed to kill *once*. *One* person. *Me!* It must think it's succeeded — stupid machine!'

Thara picked up his dead friend's axe. 'There's your wonderful Krotons for you, father!' With a yell of rage he hurled the axe at the machine. 'Murderers!'

Selris grabbed his arm. 'Thara! Don't provoke them!'

'Is that all you care about — not provoking them?'

40

'What can we do against such weapons as theirs, my son?'

The grating metallic voice boomed out once more. 'THIS IS A WARNING. YOUR LEADER HAS BEEN DESTROYED. ALL GONDS LEAVE THE LEARNING HALL AT ONCE.'

'No!' shouted Thara. 'Stay and fight!' But the death of their fellow student had taken all the fight out of the rebels.

Selris shouted, 'All of you, leave the Learning Hall. Leave now!'

The Doctor too added his persuasions. 'I think we'd all better do as they say, you know!'

Thankfully the Gonds hurried to obey. For the moment at least, the rebellion was over.

The Doctor was sitting on the bed in the alcove examining Vana's eyes with a kind of primitive opthalmascope.

Switching the instrument off, he put it to one side and began feeling the unconscious girl's skull, probing gently with sensitive fingers.

Zoe picked up the instrument and studied it, switching it on and off. It was large and clumsy, but perfectly effective. 'Where did this come from, Doctor?'

'That? Oh, I borrowed it from their scientist chap — Beta.'

'I thought the Gonds didn't know about electricity?'

'Well, they don't really. That thing works from stored solar energy. You know, Zoe, the Gonds are quite advanced in some ways. Wish they had an ETC machine though . . . '

'There are strange gaps in their knowledge. I suppose it's because they only know what the machines teach them.'

41

The Doctor straightened up, and stood looking down at Vana, who seemed to be sleeping peacefully. 'Yes, precisely. And the machines are programmed by the Krotons. So those gaps must be very significant.'

Jamie and Selris came over to them.

Selris looked down at the girl. 'How is she, Doctor?'

'Slightly better, I think. It's difficult to be sure. Selris — do you think it would be safe to go back to the Learning Hall?'

Since the attack on the Teaching Machines, everything seemed quiet, though Selris had taken the precaution of putting the Hall under guard.

'I'm not sure, Doctor? Why do you ask?'

'Oh, Zoe and I want to have another look round, don't we, Zoe?'

'Do we?'

'Yes, of course we do. Hold your hand out, Jamie.'

Puzzled, Jamie held out his hand. The Doctor took out a little phial and shook three brownish pills into his palm.

'What's all this Doctor?'

'Just some pills I got from Beta.'

'I dinna need pills. There's nothing wrong with me.'

'They're for Vana. I want you to stay here and look after her.'

Jamie looked mutinously at him. 'Why can't I come with you?'

'Because I want you to see that she swallows these pills the moment she wakes up. It's very important, Jamie. I need someone I can rely on.'

'Och, well, all right,' said Jamie, mollified.

'I shall come with you, Doctor,' announced Selris.

'My dear fellow, that's quite unnecessary.'

'I am the leader of the Gond Council. I must know what is happening.'

'Oh, well come along then. Goodbye, Jamie.'

The Doctor bustled out of the room, followed by Selris.

Jamie put a hand on Zoe's arm. 'Watch him, Zoe. You know what he's like!'

Zoe smiled understandingly. 'Don't worry, Jamie, I won't let him do anything rash!'

She hurried after the others.

The Doctor hurried down the steps that led into the Learning Hall, and came to a sudden halt, staring down at his feet. 'Aha!'

Selris stopped too. 'What?'

The big flagstone beneath the Doctor's feet had a metal ring set into the centre. 'What's this?'

'It leads to the Underhall.'

'What's down there?'

Selris shrugged. 'Nothing. It's never used.'

The Doctor glanced over at the machine, then back down at the flagstone. 'Hmm, I wonder how far down . . . ' He looked hopefully up at Selris. 'Do you think we could just take a look?'

Puzzled but obliging, Selris knelt down and heaved at the heavy flagstone. Muscles bulging with the effort, he lifted it up and moved it aside, revealing an open space and the top of a steep flight of steps.

'You stay here, Zoe,' said the Doctor. 'We shan't be long.' He disappeared down the ladder, and Selris followed.

Left on her own, Zoe wandered over to the wrecked Teaching Machine. She studied its wrecked innards for a moment, trying to reconstruct its design and purpose.

She moved on to the next Machine and studied the controls. Then, unable to resist, she reached out and pressed what she judged to be the 'on' button. The screen lit up invitingly.

43

On a sudden impulse, Zoe slipped into the curved seat, reached up and pulled down the metal helmet, fitting it over her head. Immediately a sense of pleasurable anticipation flooded her mind. She felt keen and alert, eager to begin.

A circle of complex symbols appeared on the screen, revolving in a clockwise direction. Inside it was another circle, revolving counter clockwise.

Zoe studied the complicated display for a moment. Her fingers flickered over the keyboard, resolving the symbols into a logical mathematical equation. Immediately a tremendous sense of well-being flooded over her. It was like being given the most enormous pat on the back from a favourite teacher.

The equation vanished and an even more complicated display appeared. On the side of the machine there was a calibrated dial. Its needle began climbing . . .

The dial was reproduced in the control room inside the Kroton Machine. The servo-mechanism glided forward, registering the score . . .

The Doctor looked round the vast and gloomy Underhall. He saw three shining pillars, spreading out from the ceiling overhead and disappearing into the walls and floor.

He stared thoughtfully at them. They reminded him of something . . .

His face stern as he turned to Selris. 'All right, I've seen enough.'

As he followed the Doctor up the ladder, Selris said, 'I told you there was nothing down there, Doctor.'

'But there was, Selris — something rather curious.'

'Those pillars are just the foundation of the

44

Machine.'

The Doctor wasn't listening. 'Zoe!' he called. 'What do you think you're doing?'

He ran towards her, Selris close behind him.

Zoe was still sitting at the console of the Teaching Machine, hands flickering over the keys. There was a blissful smile on her face.

Selris pulled the cap from Zoe's head, and the Doctor heaved her bodily out of the chair. She smiled vaguely at him. 'You're soon back, Doctor. I was just trying the Teaching Machine.'

'You ought to know better than to do a thing like that,' scolded the Doctor.

'But it was all so easy, Doctor — and so pleasant. The Krotons were *very* pleased with me.'

'*Pleased* with you?'

'Well . . . I *felt* they were . . . '

The Doctor clapped his hands very hard in front of Zoe's face, so she blinked and jumped back.

'Zoe, whatever these Krotons are, they are not benign and friendly. We know that, don't we?'

'Yes . . . yes, of course,' said Zoe, remembering.

'They use these machines not only to teach but to programme — to plant impressions on the mind.' The Doctor turned to Selris. 'That's how they've enslaved your people all these years.'

Selris was staring at the console in astonishment. 'Just look at that score dial, Doctor.'

'What about it?'

'It's amazing. Even our very best students register less than half that score.'

'Well, Zoe *is* something of a genius, of course. It can be very irritating at times!'

Zoe smiled.

Jamie was almost dozing off when Vana began

twisting and muttering agitatedly.

She tried to sit up. Jamie forced her gently back on the pillows. 'Now then,' he said gruffly. 'Dinna' worry, you're all right now, Vana.'

Vana's face was flushed and her eyes were wild. 'The ball,' she muttered. 'The burning ball . . . It's over my head, swallowing me up . . . '

She flattened herself against the bed, staring above her in terror.

'No, Vana, there's nothing. There's nothing here . . . '

'I saw it!' she screamed. 'I saw it!' She sat up again, writhing in terror.

To Jamie's vast relief, Thara came hurrying over. He cradled Vana in his arms, soothing her. 'It's all right. There's nothing here, Vana. You're safe.'

Vana's face twisted in terror. 'It was flashing,' she babbled feverishly. 'All the lights . . . *burning my mind . . . the lights!*' She gave one final convulsive heave, and slumped back exhausted.

Thara stroked her hair, 'Vana, you're all right now. You're home.'

Her eyes widened and she looked vaguely at him. 'Thara, is that you?'

'She recognises me,' said Thara delightedly. 'Vana, listen, nothing can hurt you now. You're going to be all right.'

She clutched his hand. 'I went into the Machine, Thara . . . '

Jamie leaned forward. 'Did you see the Krotons?'

She stared blankly at him. 'Krotons? There was just the fiery ball, flashing, coming down on me.'

Her voice rose in panic, and Thara held her tight. 'It's all right, Vana. You're safe.'

Belatedly Jamie recollected his duty. 'Here, you'd better take these. Come on, it's medicine, swallow

46

them down. Get her some water, Thara.'

Between them they managed to get her to take the pills and she soon sank back onto the pillow, her eyes closing in sleep.

Thara looked worriedly at her. 'A flashing ball, coming down on her, burning her mind . . . What did she mean? Is it another of the Kroton's weapons?'

Jamie shrugged, 'I canna' tell. You stay with her, Thara. I'm off to find the Doctor.'

The Doctor was scraping at the shining surface of the door of the Kroton Machine with an old Boy Scout jack-knife. A little way away, Zoe was doing the same thing with a nail-file. 'It's crystalline!'

The Doctor had come to the same conclusion. 'Very hard, but not brittle, I've never seen anything like it.'

Zoe nodded towards the flagstone. 'What was it like — down there?'

'Hmm? Ah yes, I saw what Selris calls the foundations. And do you know what, Zoe? It was like a *root structure*.'

'A root structure? But that would indicate . . . '

'Yes . . . That this so-called machine is organic in structure. Quite so.'

'Is that possible?'

'Why not? Some crystals do resemble simple virus forms. I wish I could get a fragment to analyse.'

'But if you're right Doctor,' said Zoe slowly, 'then this whole machine is a sort of living thing!'

'All life doesn't necessarily have feeling, you know,' began the Doctor.

He was interrupted by the boom of a gong. The Doctor winced. 'Great jumping gobstoppers, what's that?'

Selris came hurrying forward. 'It's the Krotons' signal. It means they have a message for me.'

He hurried to the circular hatch beside the door and waited. Seconds later the hatch slid open and Selris removed the inscribed plastic tablet, staring at it in amazement.

'Well,' said the Doctor impatiently, 'what does it say?'

Slowly Selris read aloud. 'Class three one nine seven . . . Selected: Female — Zoegond.'

'Zoegond?' The Doctor snatched the tablet from Selris and studied it. He looked up appalled. 'Zoe! They mean you!'

Selris looked gravely at Zoe. 'They have chosen you for a Companion of the Krotons.'

5

The Companions

The Doctor glared indignantly at Selris. 'A Companion of the Krotons? Yes, well, we all know what happens to them, don't we?'

'Oh, Doctor, what shall I do?' gasped Zoe.

'Well, Selris?' demanded the Doctor. 'She doesn't have to go — does she?'

Selris hesitated.

'Well? Does she or doesn't she?'

Reluctantly Selris said, 'I'm afraid she must, Doctor. Complete obedience is the First Law of the Krotons. If we fail to obey them, they have threatened —'

'To destroy you all, as they did before?'

Selris bowed his head. 'If you do not obey them, we shall die.'

Zoe sighed. 'Oh dear . . . '

'See what you've done?' snapped the Doctor. 'Fooling around with that ridiculous machine!'

'But I'm not a Gond!'

'Well, that stupid machine doesn't seem to know the difference. Oh well!'

The Doctor strode over to the Teaching Machine and Zoe hurried after him. 'What are you going to do?'

'Take the test of course. Can't let you go in alone. Now, what do I do?'

Zoe saw he was determined. 'First you sit down.' The Doctor sat. 'Then you put this on.' She fitted the helmet over his untidy mop of hair. 'Now, press the "on" button.'

The Doctor didn't move and Zoe realised that with the helmet covering his ears he couldn't hear her. 'Press the button!' she shouted.

'All right,' said the Doctor irritably. 'No need to shout! Now go away and don't fuss me — no, come back. What's this? It's all right, I know!'

Muttering crossly to himself, the Doctor settled himself before the console. 'Right, fire away. I'm ready.'

Nothing happened.

'The "on" button!' mouthed Zoe.

The Doctor glared at her and pressed the button.

The screen lit up. The Doctor stared indignantly at the circling symbols and began stabbing at the console. The symbols gave a final swirl, broke up and vanished.

'Doctor, you got it all wrong!' said Zoe. She glanced at the score dial, which was at its lowest reading.

'Oh dear, I was working in square roots,' grumbled the Doctor.

He leaned forward, addressing the screen. 'Can I have that again, please?'

'They don't give you a second shot,' said Zoe. 'Press the button again!'

The Doctor pressed the button and another even more complex circle of symbols appeared on the screen.

As the Doctor worked frenziedly at the console, Selris leaned forward and whispered, 'This is the most advanced Machine. Perhaps he can't answer the questions?'

'Of course he can,' said Zoe loyally. 'The Doctor's almost as clever as I am.'

Selris looked doubtfully at the score dial. 'Is he?'

Zoe leaned forward to watch the Doctor's progress, just as his second equation broke up and disappeared. 'Oh, Doctor,' she said reproachfully, 'You divided instead of multiplying. You must concentrate.'

He gave her a distracted look. 'I am, Zoe, I am.'

Frowning ferociously, the Doctor stabbed at the button once more. 'Ah, that's better.' He settled down to work.

Inside the Machine the duplicate score dial began climbing to the highest total yet achieved.

The Doctor sorted out the last and most complex equation in record time, pulled off the helmet, and sat back with a sigh of contented relief. He got out of the chair, and looked at the dial. 'I rather think I've beaten your score, Zoe.'

'You answered more questions. Anyway, it's not supposed to be a competition.'

The Doctor rubbed his temples. 'Very clever the way they make out you're pleasing them, isn't it?'

Zoe nodded. 'Perhaps they aren't as bad as we think?'

The Doctor nodded dreamily. Then he frowned. 'What?' he shouted and slapped himself hard on the head with both hands. 'Of course they are!'

It was diabolically clever, thought the Doctor. Obviously the Teaching Machines stimulated the pleasure centre of the brain so that learning was not only easy but enjoyable, and the 'approval' of the Krotons a much-desired reward. 'Well, Selris, what happens now?'

'The Krotons will be waiting for Zoe.'

'Well, they can wait. We're going in there together.'

'Normally the names don't come through for some little time.'

'Mine did,' pointed out Zoe.

Selris nodded. 'Perhaps your performance on the Teaching Machine impressed them.'

Suddenly the gong note sounded again.

'Sounds a bit like a dinner gong,' said the Doctor.

Selris hurried to the message hatch and took out the plastic square. He read out the contents. 'Class three one nine eight. Selected: Male — Doctorgond.'

'Doctorgond!' shouted the Doctor. 'Idiots!'

'It means you anyway,' said Zoe.

There was a humming sound and the door slid upwards.

The Doctor drew a deep breath. 'Well, Zoe, are you ready?'

'I suppose we really do have to?'

'We started this, so we'd better go through with it. We've got to get to the bottom of this somehow, and to do that we have to get inside.'

'It's all my fault,' said Zoe miserably.

The Doctor patted her shoulder. 'Oh, cheer up. I expect it will all be quite interesting really.'

Selris bowed his head. 'I am sorry this had to happen, Doctor. My people will always remember you.'

'What?' said the Doctor sharply. Then he realised. Selris was saying a final goodbye. As far as Selris was concerned, they were already dead.

'Yes, well that's very nice of you,' said the Doctor ironically. 'Stay close to me, Zoe.'

He took Zoe's hand and together they went into the Kroton Machine. The door slid closed behind them.

Jamie came tearing down the steps into the Learning Hall. 'Doctor! Doctor, come back!' But it was too late.

He ran up to Selris. 'What's happened?'

Selris raised his hand to hold Jamie back. Then he laid the hand on Jamie's shoulder, and gave him a look of grave sympathy. 'Your friends are gone. They have become Companions of the Krotons.'

The Doctor and Zoe moved along a darkened corridor. Every so often, a door opened before them, so that there was always only one way they could go.

The last door slid upwards, and they found themselves in a huge control room. The place was in semi-darkness, with strangely designed instrument consoles lining the walls. The only sound was the faint humming and ticking of instruments.

The Doctor had a sudden impression that the whole place was on standby. Waiting. But for what? For them, perhaps.

Zoe looked round. 'It's a space craft, isn't it, Doctor?'

'Yes, I think so, Zoe. But no crew apparently.' He raised his voice. 'Hullo! Anybody here?'

Suddenly a spotlight shone down from somewhere on high. It made a little pool of light, in the centre of which were two simple, functionally designed chairs.

'I think we've just been asked to sit down,' said Zoe nervously. They sat.

The Doctor took his watch and chain from his pocket and handed one end of the chain to Zoe. 'Hold one end of this, Zoe.'

'What for?'

The Doctor pointed upwards. Suspended above their heads was a transparent cone, packed with electronic circuitry. 'That's a force-field generator up there. The chain might help to equalise the power load.'

Zoe looked up apprehensively. 'What are they going

to do?'

Suddenly the cone began descending towards them. It glowed fiercely into life, bathing them in an almost intolerable glare.

'Doctor, I can't move,' called Zoe.

'No,' gasped the Doctor. 'Force field. Try and . . . relax.'

The revolving cone grew brighter and brighter, until it seemed to turn into a great ball of fire suspended directly above their heads.

The Doctor and Zoe writhed against the constraints of the force field, their faces twisted and distorted by the strain . . .

'*Why?*' demanded Jamie. 'Why did you let them go?'

'The Krotons commanded.'

'Och, the Krotons! They just give an order and everyone jumps, don't they? Well, I'm no' just standing here! I'm going to find a way into this box of tricks.'

Jamie began battering on the door.

Inside the Kroton control room, the pressure on Zoe and the Doctor had reached intolerable levels. They were bathed in the fierce white light from the spinning fireball above their heads. It seemed to drain all the energy from both their bodies and their brains.

Zoe was dimly aware that somehow the Doctor was helping her to bear the intolerable strain . . . The gold chain between their hands was twisting and distorting in the power-flow between them.

Inside the forcefield generator, a column of mercury was rising higher and higher. When it reached the top of the column, there was a last blinding flare of light — and everything went quiet.

'Are you all right, Zoe?' gasped the Doctor.

'Yes, I think so . . . What happened?'

The Doctor looked ruefully at his distorted watch chain. 'We were in the grip of some tremendous force . . . '

'It was tapping our mental power,' said Zoe. 'They seem to have found a way of converting mental power into energy.'

'Yes . . . I think they were using it — or rather us — to operate some kind of thermal switch.'

'Doctor, look! Over there! Wasn't there a wall in front of us?'

'Yes, there was. You know, Zoe, I think I'm beginning to understand.'

The wall that had been in front of them had vanished. In its place stood an enormous coffin-shaped transparent tank filled with some bubbling seething liquid.

In the depths of the tank, unseen as yet, a hideous shape was beginning to form . . .

6

The Krotons Awake

The Doctor rose stiffly and went over to the tank. 'Oh dear, Zoe, I think we've been and gone and done it this time!' He peered inside. 'How very curious!'

Zoe came to join him. 'We've gone and done what?'

'Just a minute, I have an idea.'

The Doctor took Beta's medicine phial from his pocket, tipped out the rest of the pills and stowed them away, and used the phial to scoop up a small quantity of the bubbling liquid. He held up the phial and peered at the contents. 'It appears to be a form of slurry, crystals in suspension.'

'What for? What's its purpose?'

'Life on your planet is supposed to have begun in the sea, hmm? Someone once called it primeval soup. Of course, there are many kinds of soup, aren't there? I wonder what this one is?' The Doctor tipped a few drops of the slurry onto a finger, tasted it cautiously and grimaced.

Zoe was looking at the tank. From the bottom there ran two long metallic hoses, each with one end plugged into the tank and the other end free. 'What do you suppose these are? They look a bit like astronauts air-lines.'

The Doctor restoppered the phial and put it in his

pocket. 'Very similar, Zoe. Yes. I think you're right.' He stared hard into the tank. 'Zoe, look!'

Inside the tank a massive shape was beginning to form. It was vaguely humanoid, yet angular and crystalline at the same time. The shape began to stir.

The Doctor jumped back. 'I think we'd better get out of here.'

He looked around. The way by which they'd come was closed now, but the way ahead seemed open. The Doctor grabbed Zoe's hand and dragged her from the control room.

As they hurried away, a huge gleaming arm, ending in a kind of clamp rose from the seething liquid in the tank and began groping vaguely at the air . . .

The Doctor and Zoe came to a corridor junction, and the Doctor paused to get his bearings.

'What are we going to do if we do get out?' asked Zoe. 'We haven't learned anything.'

The Doctor tapped the pocket holding the phial. 'Oh yes we have. Once we can analyse this . . . This way I think. Come along, Zoe!'

The huge gleaming figure climbed ponderously from the tank and stood swaying dizzily for a moment. Reaching down it groped for one of the pipes from the tank and clipped it into a socket in its body.

Immediately the creature seemed to become steadier, more alert, as if the tank was providing strength and nourishment.

Inside the tank, a second huge shape was beginning to form . . .

Jamie had abandoned his futile pounding on the door of the Kroton machine. Now he was trying to pry the doors open with his knife — with inevitably, an equal lack of success.

Selris was doing his best to dissuade him. 'I tell you,

there is no way in.'

'It's a door, isn't it?' growled Jamie. 'If I can just get it open.'

'Nobody can enter unless the Krotons wish it!'

'We'll see about that. What I need is some kind of crowbar . . .'

Jamie hunted through the Learning Hall until he found a storage alcove where a few simple tools were kept. To his joy they included a heavy crowbar. Hefting it determinedly, he strode back towards the door.

Inside the control room the second Kroton, now fully formed, was clipping its nutrient hose into place.

The Kroton Commander was adjusting controls on the scanner. 'The Gonds should be here,' observed Kroton Two in its deep grating voice.

The Kroton Commander adjusted a control on the scanner, and caught a brief glimpse of two fleeing figures. 'They are in the exit shaft.' It spoke in the same flat, emotionless tones as the other.

'Why?' demanded Kroton Two. 'They are conditioned to obey.'

'The conditioning may have failed.' The Kroton Commander jabbed at the controls with its clamp-like hand.

The Doctor and Zoe hurried through the corridors of the Kroton ship, too hurried to observe much of their strange surroundings, though Zoe was vaguely aware of glinting crystalline walls, and weirdly shaped instrument consoles.

They passed through a chamber festooned with a jungle of dangling pipes, through which gurgled multi-coloured liquids, and came at last to an ante-chamber before what the Doctor reckoned must be the

59

rear door of the ship.

The Doctor studied the door, shoving vainly at it.

'It looks as if it should slide,' said Zoe.

'There must be a trip mechanism.'

Zoe pointed to the side of the door. 'There's some sort of photo-electric cell here.' She passed her hand to and fro in front of it. 'It doesn't seem to be working.'

'And if it isn't working . . . '

'The Krotons must have cut the circuit,' concluded Zoe.

'Yes, I'm afraid so.'

'Then we're trapped, Doctor. And they know we're here.'

The Doctor began fumbling through his pockets. 'That piece of mica I picked up in the Wasteland. If I can use it to bridge the gap and trip the switch . . . '

The Doctor found the fragment of mica and began wedging it into the socket of the photo-electric cell.

Zoe looked on dubiously. 'Do you think it'll work?'

'I don't know. The whole ship's built of crystal though, so —'

The Doctor broke off as the door slid upwards with a whine of power, revealing the Wasteland outside.

Desperate to get out of the ship Zoe darted forward.

The Doctor grabbed her arm. 'Wait, Zoe — if we go out there, we'll run into those poison jets . . . '

The Kroton Commander studied the monitor. It now showed the back of the ship and the open door. 'They have re-activated the exit circuit.'

Kroton Two said matter-of-factly, 'Then the dispersion unit will kill them.'

The Kroton Commander reached for the console.

The Doctor and Zoe were still hesitating before the open door. 'We'll *have* to risk it Doctor,' said Zoe desperately. 'We can't stay here.'

The Doctor nodded. 'All right. But jump straight down from the side, Zoe. Whatever you do, don't go down the ramp . . . '

Impassively the two Krotons watched Zoe and the Doctor sprint through the open door, take a flying leap from the side of the ramp and disappear into the Wasteland. They were moving too quickly to realise that the poison spray had not been activated at all.

The Kroton Commander watched them go. 'They are not Gonds.'

'Why did you inoperate the dispersion unit?' asked Kroton Two.

'We need them alive.'

'They have now escaped,' pointed out Kroton Two.

'Keep a watch for them on all scanners. We will order the Gonds to capture them and bring them back.'

The Kroton Commander switched the scanner to the Learning Hall, where a strangely-dressed figure was trying to prise open the ship's doors with a metal bar.

'That is not a Gond either.'

'It is possible that they have evolved.'

The Kroton Commander studied the attacker.

'There has not been time. This is a similar biped animal, but it is not from this planet.'

'It is possible that these superior anthropoids have taken over the planet.'

Selris appeared on the scanner. 'That is a Gond,' said the Kroton Commander. 'Perhaps these new creatures are in alliance with the Gonds.'

'Let us take this one,' suggested Kroton Two. 'Its mind will have the capacity we need.'

61

Just as Jamie was on the point of giving up, the door of the Kroton ship slid smoothly upwards.

'At last,' said Jamie triumphantly.

'No, don't enter,' warned Selris.

Jamie brandished his crowbar. 'Dinna worry, I've got this!'

Pushing Selris aside Jamie disappeared inside the ship. The door closed behind him.

Like the Doctor and Zoe, Jamie found himself unavoidably led to the central control room. But as he stepped inside, crowbar at the ready, two vast angular shapes bore down on him.

Jamie swung round in amazement. The creatures were enormous, almost twice the size of a man. They had huge barrel shaped torsos, high ridged shoulders and a solid base on which they seemed to slide like hovercraft. The massive arms ended in giant clamps. The most terrifying of all were the heads, blank, many faceted and rising to a point in a shape like that of a giant crystal.

Despite their robotic features there was something crystalline about the giant creatures as though they had been grown rather than made . . .

Before Jamie could even think of resisting, Kroton Two reached out with surprising speed, the clamp-hand fastening about his neck, choking him into semi-consciousness.

The creature moved Jamie effortlessly across the control room and deposited him on one of the chairs.

The two giant forms looked dispassionately down at him.

'Have you damaged it?' asked the Kroton Commander.

'No. It is alive.'

'Animal tissue is fragile,' reminded the Kroton

Commander.

Jamie writhed in the chair, gasping to get his breath back.

'It is recovering,' said Kroton Two. 'Test its mind.'

Jamie regained full consciousness to find himself in the grip of some invisible force. A burning ball revolved just above his head, sucking energy from his body and his mind. Held in the grip of the force-field Jamie's body jerked convulsively, his face distorted with the unbearable strain, while the two giant forms watched his agony unmoved.

The Kroton Commander studied a reading on a nearby instrument panel. 'This is not a high brain,' it observed dispassionately. 'It is a primitive.'

Kroton Two spoke with an equal lack of emotion. 'Then the power will kill it!'

Jamie writhed in the chair . . .

7

The Militants

The Kroton Commander reached out a clamped hand, and touched controls.

The fireball rose higher and faded away, and the invisible force released its hold. 'It is still of value. It can give us information about the other creatures.'

The Commander gestured towards the monitor, which showed the Doctor and Zoe hurrying away across the Wasteland.

As they hurried along, Zoe came to a sudden stop. 'This isn't the way to the Gond city, Doctor.'

'Of course it isn't. It's the way to the TARDIS!'

'The TARDIS? But we can't leave Jamie behind.'

'I need to use the TARDIS laboratory, Zoe. And don't worry about Jamie, he's quite safe. He's looking after Vana, isn't he? Now do come along . . . '

Jamie looked up at the two nightmare figures looming above him.

A voice boomed, 'Where are you from?'

'Och, are you two still here? I thought I'd dreamed you up!'

'Where are you from?'

'What? Oh, Earth.'

'You are of the same race as these bipeds?'

The Kroton gestured towards the monitor screen.

Jamie peered at the screen and grinned. 'Zoe — and the Doctor! Where are they?'

'You are space travellers?'

Jamie was looking intently at the scanner, 'They're in the Wasteland. They got out, then! Good old Doctor — ouch!' He yelled as a clamp-hand closed on his upper arm in a bone-crushing grip.

'Answer!' boomed Kroton Two.

'You're breaking my shoulder!'

'Do not damage the creature,' said the Commander reprovingly.

The crushing grip relaxed.

The Commander repeated the question. 'You and these other creatures are space travellers?'

'Ay, that's right.'

Kroton Two said, 'Look, Commander.'

Both Krotons studied the monitor screen, which now showed the Doctor and Zoe about to enter the TARDIS. The Commander swung round on Jamie. 'What is that?'

'It's called the TARDIS.'

'What is its function?'

'It travels through time and space,' said Jamie. This was the sum total of his knowledge about the TARDIS.

Kroton Two moved to another control console, and suddenly a spinning vortex of light overlaid the two figures outside the TARDIS. 'Range zero seven. Dispersion unit on target.'

On the monitor screen, Zoe was just approaching the TARDIS door, the Doctor close behind her. 'If that object is their space craft Commander, then they are leaving. Shall I open fire?'

Jamie leaned forward urgently. 'They're not

leaving. They wouldn't — not without me . . . '

Beta's laboratory was a long, low, cluttered room. It was a curious mixture of the primitive and the technologically advanced — rather like that of a medieval alchemist who had discovered a few basic scientific truths. Barrels and tubs and jars of all shapes and sizes were everywhere.

Beta was busily pouring liquid from a beaker into a hanging bowl, which was suspended over a blazing oil burner, when suddenly he heard the sound of marching feet.

Beta looked up guiltily. He was conducting a simple chemical experiment, and all chemical study had been strictly forbidden by the Krotons.

If someone had informed on him . . .

Suddenly Beta's laboratory was filled with pike-wielding guards. They seemed to be led by Eelek, deputy leader of the Council, and Axus, his chief henchman.

They made a curious pair, thought Beta. Eelek round-faced and bland, with his smooth oily manner, and the fierce, sharp-faced Axus, Captain of the Guard.

Carefully setting down his beaker, Beta looked up. 'You wish to see me?'

Eelek gave his faintly sinister smile. 'Yes. You received my message?'

'I heard only that the Council required my advice. On a matter of science, I presume?'

'No. On a matter of war.'

'War?'

'Against the Krotons.'

'War against the Krotons?' Beta turned away dismissively. 'You must both be out of your minds.'

Axus grabbed his shoulder and swung him around.

67

'Now just you listen to me, Beta —'

'No!' snapped Eelek. 'We don't have to resort to that — not yet.'

Sulkily Axus let go of Beta's arm.

Beta decided it was time to be diplomatic. 'Of course I'll listen. There's no need for us to quarrel.'

'You're a scientist, Beta,' said Eelek. 'Surely you, of all people, want to be free — free of the Krotons?'

'Free, yes,' said Beta. 'Dead, no.'

'But we can defeat them, Beta.'

'Can we? Our ancestors tried.'

'They were savages, primitive men with clubs and axes.'

Supporting his leader, Axus gestured around the laboratory. 'We're much more advanced now. Look at all this!'

'Are we?' said Beta bitterly. 'All our knowledge was given to us — by the Krotons.'

Eelek smiled. 'Then let us use it against them.'

'You're talking nonsense, Eelek,' said Beta despairingly. 'I tell you, we know only what the Krotons tell us. We don't think, we obey.'

Axus looked disgustedly at Eelek. 'He could help us — if only he wasn't afraid of the Krotons.'

'Don't you think I *want* to be free of them?' shouted Beta. 'Don't you think I'd like to discover truth for myself instead of being fed knowledge as a dog is fed scraps?'

'Well then — will you help us? Make new weapons?'

'To attack the Krotons?' Sadly Beta shook his head. 'I spent some time talking to the stranger — the Doctor. He made me realise how pitifully little the Krotons have told us. Now, if he would help —'

'You can forget about the Doctor *and* his friend,' said Eelek maliciously.

'What do you mean?'

'They submitted themselves to the Teaching Machines in the Learning Hall. They scored the highest results ever recorded.'

Axus said, 'Naturally the Krotons summoned them. They went into the Machine.'

'So, by now they must be dead,' said Eelek dismissively. 'Now, Beta, *will you help us?*'

'Perhaps . . . but you must give me time. There are certain things the Krotons forbid us to study, deadly fluids that eat away flesh, and even metal. In time I could develop a way of attacking them . . . '

'In time,' sneered Eelek. 'Oh yes. It's always "in time" isn't it? Just be patient, just wait for a little more time . . . '

'We've been slaves for a thousand years, Eelek. Do you really think you can free us in one day?'

'Yes,' said Eelek arrogantly.

'At least wait and see what Selris has to say.'

'From now on, you will no longer obey Selris. You will obey me.'

All at once, Beta understood. This wasn't so much a revolution against the Krotons as an internal coup, directed against Selris. Eelek had always been ambitious. Now he was taking over.

The Krotons were staring impassively at the monitor screen, which showed the TARDIS sitting in the Wasteland.

'The space craft may leave at any time, Commander,' reminded Kroton Two. 'Shall I fire?'

The Commander switched off the aiming device. 'No. We cannot kill them. We still need their minds. You will leave the Dynotrope and fetch them back.'

Kroton Two moved to the central tank and unclipped the connecting pipe. From a storage place behind the tank he produced a small portable cylinder, which he clipped in its place.

Jamie was watching all this with the keenest interest. They needed the stuff in the tank to stay alive. If he could cut off their supply . . .

The Kroton moved slowly to the door, pausing by the entrance to take a sort of hand-cannon from a rack by the wall. The weapon fitted on to its hand as an extension.

As the second Kroton moved through the doorway, Jamie turned and looked quickly at the Kroton Commander. It was hunched over the control panel, seemingly forgetting that he was there.

Jamie began sliding cautiously from his chair. There was a second weapon in the rack. Suddenly the Kroton swung around. 'What is the operating principle of your craft?'

'The what? Och, you mean how does it work? Only the Doctor knows that!'

'What is its transference interval?'

Jamie gave the Kroton a baffled look. 'Transference interval? What's that?'

The Kroton turned away dismissively. 'You have no value.'

The voice of Kroton Two came from the console. 'Vision control required now.'

Was there a hint of panic in the grating voice, Jamie wondered? Maybe the monsters weren't happy outside their precious machine. If he could get one in the open . . .

On the monitor screen he saw Kroton Two standing at the top of the ramp, just outside the now open rear door — the one that led to the Wasteland.

The Commander operated controls. 'Vision control on, Proceed.'

Jamie watched as the giant creature moved

cautiously down the ramp and out into the Wasteland, the massive cannon held out before it. It was almost, thought Jamie, as if the thing were nervous . . .

Thara was sitting by the sleeping Vana, when Selris returned. 'How is she?'

'Better, much better, but very tired. I'm sure she'll be all right by morning though.'

'That is good news,' said Selris heavily, and sank onto a couch.

Thara looked up, surprised by his father's tone. All of a sudden, Selris looked weary — weary and old. Thara was used to thinking of Selris as a sort of invincible iron man, and he was shocked to see his father show signs of human weakness.

'Where are the strangers, Father? Still in the Learning Hall?'

'Gone,' said Selris wearily.

'You mean they've left? Gone back to wherever they came from?'

Selris shook his head. 'They went into the Machine. The Krotons sent for Zoe, and the Doctor insisted on going with her.'

Thara stared at him in astonishment. 'And you let them go? Why didn't you stop them?'

'What could I do, my son? It was the will of the Krotons.'

'But why didn't they run? They could have escaped in their machine. They must have known what would happen to them.'

'They did,' said Selris slowly. 'But they also knew what would happen to us, to our race, if the Krotons' order was not obeyed.' He rose. 'I must go. There is a meeting of the Council.'

'That's all you ever think about,' accused Thara. 'Holding meetings, talking . . . How about *acting*?'

'Against the Krotons?'

'Yes! Against the Krotons. You still think of them as our benefactors, don't you?'

'No. I think of them as enemies. As enemies against whom we are completely powerless.'

'Well, Eelek is going to do something about it —'

Vana stirred and moaned.

Thara lent over her. 'It's all right, Vana you're quite safe now.'

'I feel weak,' she murmured. 'So weak . . . '

'It's all right,' said Thara soothingly. 'We're looking after you.'

She drifted slowly back into sleep.

Jamie was watching events in the control room — and awaiting his chance.

The Kroton Commander had its back turned. It was leaning over the instrument console, tracking and guiding the progress of Kroton Two, who could be seen on the monitor, marching across the Wasteland.

Jamie slipped out of his chair and stood up. If he could reach one of the doors . . .

The Kroton Commander swung round. 'Do not move!'

Hurriedly, Jamie slipped back into his chair. 'I was only stretching my legs . . . Look, what are you going to do with me?'

'You are of no value.'

'What's that supposed to mean?'

The Kroton said dismissively, 'You are of no value, therefore you will be dispersed.'

'Dispersed?' thought Jamie. 'What does that mean?'

Then he realised. He wasn't a magician like the Doctor or a genius like Zoe. He could tell the Krotons nothing they wanted to know — so he was of no further use to them.

He was to be dispersed — destroyed. Reduced to ashes that would blow away in the wind — like that first unfortunate Gond they had seen stagger from the Machine . . .

8

The Attack

Father and son glared at each other, over the sleeping form of Vana.

Thara sighed. Despite a very real affection for each other, he and his father seemed doomed to quarrel. If only Selris wasn't so fixed in his opinions, so sure he was always right. Thara smiled wryly. Or perhaps it was because they were so much alike.

It was Selris who spoke first. 'Thara! What did you mean — about Eelek?'

'I meant that you haven't realised what is going on, Father. Eelek is no longer your deputy. He's taken over as Leader of the Council.'

'But he has no authority . . . '

'A vote was taken, Father,' said Thara wearily. 'Everyone in the City knows how the Krotons have been tricking us. Eelek announced it!'

Selris was appalled. 'The fool. The people will want revenge.'

'Exactly. And that's what Eelek has promised them.'

'But can't you see? Doesn't he care what happens to our people?'

'Eelek says he is a patriot,' said Thara drily.

Selris nodded, beginning to see what had happened.

Eelek had always been ambitious — and he was a politician. When obedience to the Krotons had been the accepted line, no-one had been more slavish then Eelek, more insistent on scrupulously obeying every rule.

But now the mood of the people had changed, and Eelek had seized his chance. The people wanted war, and they would only follow a leader who promised to give it to them. Follow him to their graves, thought Selris bitterly.

'It is not patriotism to lead people into a war they cannot win.'

Thara shrugged. 'Maybe Eelek is right. We can't allow the Krotons to rule us forever without putting up a fight.'

'One day, my son, we will be strong enough to fight them.'

'When?' asked Thara cynically. 'After another thousand years?'

'Eelek must be stopped,' said Selris broodingly.

'How? He's not going to listen to you, Father. And nor will anyone else. Our people want this war . . . because of what happened to Vana and the others.'

'And how is Eelek going to fight the Krotons? Lead a march on their machine?'

'Have you got a better idea?'

Selris sat brooding for a moment. Thara was quite right. In their present mood the Gonds wouldn't follow a leader who spoke of peace, of caution and moderation.

So, if there had to be an attack on the Krotons, decided Selris, then he, not Eelek would lead it. It was the only way to re-establish his position as leader. And Selris had ruled too long to give up power lightly.

'There is one way we could fight them,' said Selris at last. 'By not letting them know they were being attacked . . . '

The Kroton Commander was still tracking and guiding its fellow Kroton on the journey through the Wasteland. 'Radius one seven nine. Vector five.'

Jamie leaned forward in his seat. 'What about the Doctor and Zoe? What are you going to do with them?'

'They are needed for the Dynotrope.'

Jamie looked around him. 'The Dynotrope? That's this machine, is it?'

The Kroton Commander's attention was back on the monitor screen, which now showed the viewpoint of the second Kroton stumbling cautiously through the Wasteland. 'Radius one six eight. Vector four.'

'Well, why does this Dynotrope of yours need them?' persisted Jamie. 'And why have you been killing off the Gonds?'

The Krotons seemed to have little objection to answering questions, thought Jamie. He might as well gather all the information he could. Besides, if he could keep it talking it might forget about dispersing him, at least for a time.

'The Dynotrope needs high brains for transfer power. The Gonds have no high brains, and despite our conditioning they have not succeeded in evolving them.'

'And that makes it all right to kill them, does it?'

'That is procedure,' said the Kroton flatly. 'Radius one six three. Vector Four.'

Beta was still trying to persuade Eelek to delay his attack on the Krotons. 'Selris should be here before any decision is taken,' he argued. 'He is the leader of the Council — or am I mistaken?'

'You are mistaken,' said Axus smugly.

'But Selris is old and wise. In time of war we need a strong experienced leader.'

'Eelek has taken over,' announced Axus.

Beta turned to Eelek. 'So you've achieved your ambition at last.'

Eelek drew himself up. 'I have the support of the entire Council.'

'I see. It must be quite a change for you to feel popular, Eelek.'

Eelek smiled evilly. 'There is a limit to what I will stand from you, Beta.'

Beta laughed. 'I wonder if you'll still be popular when hundreds of our people have been killed? Do you want to provoke a repetition of the massacre we suffered when the Krotons first arrived?'

'Things have changed since then, Beta,' sneered Eelek. 'Or hadn't you noticed? Today we have fireballs, slings, machines that can smash the strongest buildings to rubble.'

'Have you ever really looked at the Wasteland?' asked Beta wearily. 'Nothing grows there, even to this day. It smells of death. Compared with their weapons we still have only clubs and stones!'

'Come on, now,' said Jamie persuasively. 'What have I ever done to harm you? How would you like to die without knowing the reason, eh?'

He was addressing the broad back of the Commander, who was still busy at the console. As he spoke, Jamie was edging slowly towards the rack from which the other Kroton had taken its weapon.

'Krotons cannot die,' announced the Commander impassively.

'What's that? You mean you can't be killed?' said Jamie in horror. 'You live for ever?'

'We function permanently unless we exhaust.'

'And what do you mean by exhaust?'

'The exhaustion procedure is merely a reversion to basic molecules. But the matter can be re-animated.'

'What about me though?' said Jamie indignantly. 'I can't be re-animated. Why do you want to kill me? What good will it do you?'

'All waste matter must be dispersed,' said the Kroton chillingly. 'That is procedure.'

Jamie edged a little closer to the weapon.

The TARDIS door opened and the Doctor and Zoe emerged. The Doctor was carrying his little phial in one hand and a carpet bag in the other. He handed the phial to Zoe while he closed the TARDIS door.

'So, the life system of these creatures is based on tellurium, eh? Fascinating, isn't it, Zoe? And that tank was obviously some kind of polarised centrifuge.'

'Which *we* activated,' said Zoe bitterly.

The Doctor beamed. 'Oh, you mustn't blame yourself, Zoe. The Kroton Machine must have been there for thousands of years waiting for someone as clever as us to come along!'

'Just like a giant mousetrap,' said Zoe sadly. 'And those poor Gond students have been the mice.'

The Doctor frowned. 'Yes, that's horrible. Still you must admit that the Krotons have found a very good way of surviving through time . . . '

The Doctor went to an outcrop of rock just beside the TARDIS and began sorting through the fragments of loose stone at its base.

Zoe looked on in mild surprise. 'What are you doing, Doctor?'

'There are some rather splendid sulphur deposits just about here.'

Zoe smiled. 'Jamie was complaining about the smell as soon as we arrived.'

'Hydrogen telluride!'

'What? Oh yes, of course. The worst smell in the world!'

'In any world,' agreed the Doctor.

'Doctor — what do you want sulphur for?'

The Doctor looked up almost guiltily. 'What? Oh it might just come in useful. Very useful stuff, sulphur . . . '

Zoe looked round uneasily. There was nothing to see except the bleak grey Wasteland all around. But all the same . . .

'You know, Doctor, I keep getting a feeling we're being *watched*.'

The Doctor was busy throwing chunks of rock into his carpet bag . . .

Jamie could see Zoe's worried face on the monitor screen in the Kroton control room.

'Radius two zero. Vector one. Object in range.'

Which presumably meant that the second Kroton was very close, thought Jamie. He leaned forward urgently, willing his friends to hear him.

'Get back,' he muttered. 'Get back in the TARDIS!' But they couldn't hear him. Clearly it was up to him. Carefully, he lifted the remaining laser cannon from the rack.

The Doctor picked up a chunk of crumbly rock. 'Look at this! Almost pure sulphur.'

'Very nice, Doctor. Can we go now?'

'Very shortly. What do you know about tellurium?'

Zoe's computer-like mind came into operation. 'Well, it's one of the exceptional elements in the periodic table. Its atomic weight is one hundred and twenty-eight, its atomic number fifty-two —'

Suddenly Zoe dried up.

'Go on,' urged the Doctor.

Zoe gulped. 'It doesn't seem to matter anymore. Look, Doctor!'

The Doctor looked. 'My giddy aunt!'

A Kroton stood regarding them from the top of a nearby ridge. It began gliding towards them, covering them with a kind of bulbous weapon — a laser-cannon, guessed the Doctor. And at that range there wasn't the slightest chance of escape.

'You will return to the Dynotrope,' announced the Kroton.

The Doctor rose cautiously to his feet, clutching his carpet bag. 'Er yes, yes of course . . . I mean, if you insist . . . '

'Return!' boomed the Kroton.

The Doctor took Zoe's hand.

The Kroton Commander was totally intent on the scene on the monitor so Jamie seized his chance. He heaved up the massive weapon and trained it on the Commander.

Alerted by the sounds of his movement, the Kroton swung round. 'Stop!'

His fighting blood up, Jamie yelled, 'Now we'll see if you die or not!'

Somehow he managed to find the firing stud in the base of the weapon and the laser beam poured from the muzzle, like flame from a flame thrower.

The Kroton staggered back. 'Stop!' it called. 'St-o-op.' Its voice became slurred like a slowed-down tape . . .

Suddenly the energy blast faltered and began to die away. Immediately the Kroton recovered and began advancing on Jamie again . . .

Jamie stabbed frantically at the firing button but it was no use. Clearly whatever power source charged

81

the weapon was exhausted.

The Kroton bore down on him. He hurled the weapon at it, but with absolutely no effect.

The Kroton came steadily onwards, massive, unstoppable, a living tank. Clamp-like hands reached out. Jamie dodged beneath them, but the sheer bulk of the creature knocked him back. His head thudded into the wall and he slid half-dazed to the ground.

A frantic voice came from the console. 'Commander! Direction point! I have lost contact.'

Turning away from Jamie, the Commander moved back towards the console.

To their astonishment, the Doctor and Zoe saw the muzzle of the laser-cannon wavering to and fro.

The Kroton itself was staggering helplessly. 'Direction point. Direction point required immediately.'

The Doctor grabbed Zoe's hand. 'Quick, Zoe, run. Over there!' He pointed towards an overhanging rock a little way up the slope. They began to run.

The Commander was bringing the wandering Kroton back under control. 'Radius one zero. Vector three.'

'Do I proceed, Commander?'

'The auto-scanner has lost contact with the aliens. You will destroy their TARDIS machine. They must not escape.'

'Direction point?'

'Radius four-one. Vector two.'

Crouched behind the rock, the Doctor and Zoe watched the Kroton's stumbling progress towards the TARDIS. 'Can't it see?' whispered Zoe.

'Apparently not in this light. It was pretty dark in the Machine, remember.'

'It's moving now. Look, it seems to be going towards the TARDIS.'

'Yes . . . yes . . . I rather think it's being directed by the Kroton Machine's scanners. They must have put up a spy satellite . . . '

The Kroton came level with the TARDIS, raised the laser cannon and fired. A stream of fierce white light poured from the muzzle, and the TARDIS was enveloped in a fiery glow.

When the glow faded, the TARDIS had disappeared.

9

The Second Attack

'Doctor,' gasped Zoe. 'The TARDIS! It's gone!'

'Mmm, yes,' said the Doctor absently, apparently not in the least concerned.

'Now what shall we do?'

'Not much we can do, my dear, until that wretched Kroton goes away.'

The Kroton was standing motionless, as if waiting for orders.

The voice of Kroton Two crackled from the console. 'Further instructions?'

'Return to the Dynotrope.'

'Direction point?'

'Reverse previous readings.'

Jamie meanwhile had recovered conciousness and was considering his next move. He raised himself up on one elbow, and saw the Kroton Commander start to swing round.

Jamie slumped down again. The Kroton looked at him for a moment then, apparently satisfied that he was dead, or at least unconscious, returned its attention to he console.

The Doctor and Zoe watched from hiding as the

Kroton turned and moved slowly away, disappearing at last behind the rocks.

Suddenly Zoe heard a strange, unmistakable sound — the characteristic wheezing and groaning of a TARDIS materialisation. And sure enough, the TARDIS was materialising. Suddenly there it was, not in the spot where it had disappeared, but quite close at hand, perched precariously on a spur of rock.

'It's back, Doctor,' exclaimed Zoe delightedly. 'Look, it's all right!'

'Yes, I know . . . Dear me, what a stupid place to land! You can tell the captain's not at the helm, can't you?'

Zoe looked at him accusingly. 'You *knew!* You knew it would come back like that, didn't you?'

'Well, yes actually.' The Doctor smiled. 'Mind you, it only does that if I remember to set the HADS.'

'The what?'

'The HADS, Zoe. Hostile Action Displacement Service. When the HADS is operating, the TARDIS automatically dematerialises, and then comes back when it thinks the danger's over.'

Zoe looked at him curiously, realising how often the Doctor talked about the TARDIS as if it were a living being.

The Doctor stood up. 'I think it's safe to go now.'

'Go where?'

'Well, we must let the Gonds know we're all right, mustn't we? And Jamie will be worried too.'

They moved away.

In Beta's laboratory the argument was still raging. 'I tell you it's simple,' Eelek was saying. 'First we destroy the Learning Hall, then we make a frontal attack.'

'Madness,' said Beta flatly. 'Suicide.'

'What does a Controller of Science know of war?' said Axus contemptuously.

'You came here asking my advice and, as Controller of Science, I've given it. Wait till we can develop effective weapons.'

'And how long will that take?' demanded Eelek. 'I say attack now!'

'No, Eelek,' said a deep, authoritative voice.

With a sigh of relief, Beta saw Selris stride into the room. 'You'll be pleased to know, Selris, that Eelek has taken your place!'

Selris said scornfully. 'To lead you in an attack on the Krotons?'

Eelek drew himself up. 'That is my plan.'

'I forbid it,' said Selris.

He spoke with such authority that for a moment Eelek was daunted. Then he recovered, his voice loud and angry. '*You* can't forbid anything.' He turned to Axus. 'Order the slings and fireballs to be prepared.'

Axus led the guards out of the room.

Eelek gave Selris a triumphant look. 'We've heard enough of your plans,' he said and followed his supporter.

Beta shook his head. 'Slings and fireballs! They'll never reach the Krotons while they're still in that machine.'

To Beta's astonishment, Selris said, 'Exactly, Beta. Now, I have a plan that will draw them out. Under the Hall of Learning, there are three pillars which support the machine . . . '

Jamie was still shamming dead on the floor of the Kroton control room. He was beginning to wonder how much longer he could get away with it.

Luckily the return of the second Kroton had provided a distraction. For the moment the two Krotons were absorbed in the monitor screen over the console.

'The high brains must be recaptured before exhaust time!' the Commander was saying.

'The alien craft is now dispersed,' said Kroton Two.

'Check exhaust time.' The Commander operated the controls. 'Commence check. Lineal power static?'

'Static.'

'Gravitation feed?'

'Normal.'

'Auxilliary output?'

'Rising.'

Jamie decided that this was the moment. He rose cautiously and crept silently towards the exit. Behind him the voices of the Krotons were still booming out.

'Dynotrope balance?'

'Balance — four.'

The Kroton Commander checked the final readings. He turned to his companion and said emotionlessly. 'The Dynotrope will exhaust in three hours.'

At Selris's house, Thara and Vana were packing food, clothing and equipment into a simple backpack.

'Are you sure you're strong enough for the journey?' asked Thara solicitously.

Vana smiled. 'Of course I am. I keep telling you, I'm all right now.'

And indeed, after several hours more sleep, Vana had woken up more or less restored to normal.

Thara had no idea whether it was the Doctor's hypnotism, Beta's medicine, or simply the restorative effects of sleep. He was just thankful to see Vana herself again.

'I can carry you, you know,' he said tenderly.

'There's no need — I can walk!'

'It's a long way to the hills —' Thara broke off as the Doctor and Zoe entered. 'Doctor, you're back!'

'That's right,' said the Doctor cheerfully. 'Sorry we took so long.'

'We thought you were dead! Selris said you'd gone into the Machine.'

'Oh, quite. Yes, we did actually. But what goes in must come out, you know.' He beamed at Vana. 'You're better, aren't you?'

'Much better, Doctor.'

'Good, good!' The Doctor looked at the supplies. 'Well, I hope you have a nice holiday. It looks as if you're going away.'

'We are. But not for a holiday. Didn't you know? The city is being evacuated.'

The Doctor stared at him, a terrible suspicion forming in his mind. 'Just a minute — *why* is the City being evacuated?'

'Father is leading a party to attack the Krotons. He hopes they'll come out into the open so we can strike back.'

'Oh no!' groaned the Doctor. 'Didn't he learn his lesson last night, when you attacked the Teaching Machines?'

'You don't understand, Doctor. Selris has a plan. They're going to strike the Machine from underneath, attack the supports.'

The Doctor leaped to his feet. 'I don't think that's a very good idea! Come along, Zoe! Thara would you mind taking us to Beta? At once, please!'

Before anyone really knew what was happening, the Doctor had bustled them all out of the room.

Selris had managed to assemble a sizeable team of

workmen from those Gonds still loyal to him. Now he stood in the Underhall watching the results of their work with grim satisfaction.

A team of labourers had lifted the flagstones and dug away the earth from around the base of the main supporting pillar.

Gond engineers had fixed an enormous chain around the pillar. The chain in turn was attached to a primitive but immensely powerful form of winch, used by Gond farmers for dragging out gnarled tree stumps when they were clearing new fields. The winch stood close by with a team of brawny Gond workers ready to turn the cast iron cog-wheel that powered it.

Selris raised his hand. 'We're ready for the stump draver now.'

The labourers bent their backs to their work. The chain around the pillar began to draw taut . . .

Beta looked up from a bubbling retort as the Doctor bustled into the laboratory, followed by the others. 'If you've come to try to persuade me to leave, Thara, you're wasting your time.'

'I haven't,' said Thara. 'The Doctor wanted to see you — and your laboratory.'

'Oh?' said Beta suspiciously.

The Doctor looked round, rubbing his hands. 'Splendid, splendid! My dear Beta, I just wondered if you could do a little job for me?'

He tipped a pile of yellow crumbly rock from his carpet bag onto one of Beta's work benches.

Beta looked at it with distaste. 'What's all this?'

'Sulphur,' said the Doctor simply. He fished a crumpled scrap of paper from his pocket. 'I've written out the instructions here — I don't know if you can follow them?'

He looked on anxiously as Beta studied the paper.

'Yes, I think so,' said Beta a little doubtfully. 'The Krotons have forbidden us to study chemistry.'

'Exactly,' said the Doctor. 'And Beta, did it ever occur to you to wonder why?'

'Where's Jamie, Doctor?' asked Zoe suddenly. She turned to Vana. 'I've just realised, he was supposed to be looking after you. He wasn't there, and he isn't here, so where's he got to?'

There was a moment of silence. Then Thara said, 'But we thought *you* knew where he was. He followed you to the Learning Hall.'

Zoe said, 'Suppose he tried to get into the Machine?'

'Just what he would do,' agreed the Doctor. 'We'd better go and look for him.' He paused in the doorway. 'Beta, you'll let me have a sample of that as soon as possible won't you?' Then he was gone.

'We'd better be going ourselves, Vana,' said Thara.

She shook her head. 'I'm a scientist too, remember. I'm going to stay and help Beta.'

'Oh no, you're not. You're going up into the hills, the pair of you,' said Beta.

But Vana was as obstinate as she was beautiful. 'Don't be ridiculous, Beta,' she said calmly. 'We're not leaving you here.' She sat down on a stool. 'Besides I'm beginning to feel quite faint again, I don't think I could walk another step!'

Beta smiled. 'All right.' He handed her the instructions. 'We'll make a start.'

Inside their control room the usually emotionless Krotons were in a state of panic, so much so that their heads were literally spinning.

'The gravitational feed is dropping,' shouted the Commander.

'The Dynotrope is moving out of balance,' said

91

Kroton Two.

'Switch static feed to full volume.'

'Full volume on!'

Their heads stopped spinning as the Krotons regained control.

'Commence systems check,' ordered the Commander.

When the Doctor and Zoe came down into the Underhall the whole place was shuddering with the movement of the great central column, which was vibrating like a plucked guitar-string.

'Shine a light up there,' ordered Selris suddenly.

The light of a hand toch revealed a huge crack in the hall's upper wall.

'If that goes the whole place will come down,' shouted one of the Gond engineers.

'The Machine will come down first,' said Selris grimly.

The Doctor was horrified at what he saw. 'Stop it! Stop it at once, you idiots! Can't you see what you're doing?'

He ran over to the chain. 'Unhook this thing. You're meddling with forces you don't understand!'

Suddenly there was a low rumbling from above and the whole section of roof around the pillar suddenly gave way.

'Look out, Doctor!' called Zoe.

The Doctor shoved Zoe towards the stairs. 'Run, Zoe run!' But although the Doctor managed to push Zoe clear, he was too late to save himself.

Zoe turned to make sure he was following, just in time to see a shower of dust and rubble cascade from the ceiling, burying the Doctor . . .

10

Battle Plans

Zoe tried to go to the Doctor's aid, but another shower of falling rubble drove her back, and she collapsed at the bottom of the steps, coughing and choking.

Thara and Vana hurried down the stairs into the Learning Hall, and stopped, appalled by the devastation before them. Many of the stone pillars were smashed, great chunks of the floor had simply fallen away, and the Teaching Machines were half buried in rubble. However, the hatch that led to the Underhall was still clear.

Thara turned to Vana. 'You stay here. I must find out what's happening below.'

He began picking his way across between the pile of rubble and disappeared down the narrow stair.

'Be careful,' called Vana, but he was already out of sight.

Struggling to her feet, Zoe found Thara beside her.

'Zoe! Are you all right?'

'Yes, I think so. No bones broken anyway!'

'This way then. I'd better get you out.' He took her arm.

Zoe pulled away. 'No, we've got to find the

Doctor . . . '

'Where is he?'

'Somewhere over there, by the base of the pillar . . . '

They began picking their way through the rubble.

Returning to the Learning Hall to assess the damage, Selris was astonished to find Vana waiting by the open hatch.

'Vana! What are you doing here? Why aren't you in the hills?'

Vana held out a stone phial. 'Thara and I stayed to help Beta make some acid. We were bringing some here for the Doctor when we felt the earthquake.'

'Where is the Doctor?'

'He's probably buried somewhere down there.'

The Doctor had been buried, but, as it happened, not too deeply. Thara found him, just inside the pit at the base of the column fighting his way out from under a coating of rubble.

Luckily the really big chunks of falling masonry had missed him, and although he was dirty and dusty and cross, the Doctor was quite unhurt.

'Here he is,' yelled Thara. 'I've found him!' He jumped into the pit and helped the Doctor to his feet.

Zoe came running up. 'Doctor? Are you all right?'

'Oh yes, I think so. Nothing seems to be broken.'

Thara helped him to climb out. 'Come along, then, you two, we must hurry. There could be another collapse any minute!'

Although the vibrating of the column had lessened, it had by no means stopped and there were ominous creaks and cracking sounds from overhead.

'Yes, I know,' shouted the Doctor. 'If they don't stabilise that machine soon . . . Thara, look out!'

As Thara had predicted there was indeed another collapse. More chunks of rubble showered down from the ceiling, and this time it was not the Doctor but Thara who was the victim.

The falling rubble knocked him to the ground, and a huge chunk of rock fell across his leg, pinning him down.

Now it was the Doctor's turn to be the rescuer. 'Don't worry, I'll get you out!' he called. 'Zoe, give me a hand.'

He began heaving at the rock, and Zoe came forward to help him. With a mighty effort they started to lift the rock free from Thara's leg.

The Krotons were still struggling desperately to restore the equilibrium of their machine.

'Cut auxiliaries!' ordered the Commander.

'Auxiliaries cut.'

'Feed-in emergency power. Gravitation feed check?'

'Gravitation feed static.'

The flashing warning lights winked out one by one, and the high-pitched scream of the vibration died away.

The Kroton Commander studied the readings. 'Dynotrope balance normal.'

It operated the scanner controls, and the monitor showed a view of the central column. The Krotons studied the pit, now filled with rubble, the half-buried bodies of the Gond labourers, and finally the column itself, which had split clear down the middle.

'The Gonds have attacked the Dynotrope,' said Kroton Two.

The Krotons never had any worries about stating the obvious. Indeed their whole conversation consisted of a series of such statements.

The monitor picked up the Doctor and Zoe, deep in

conversation with Thara. The Kroton Commander said, 'There are the two high brains. Bring them here.'

Helped by some of the surviving Gond workers, the Doctor and Zoe had carried Thara up into the Learning Hall to a clear space by the bottom of the steps, where the wounded were being cared for.

Zoe ran her hands along Thara's leg. 'It could be a fracture, and it's badly cut and bruised. Better keep it still for a while. Give me that wood, will you, Doctor?'

The Doctor watched in admiration as Zoe bandaged Thara's leg, and fixed it in a rough splint. 'Well done, Zoe. But as soon as you've finished we ought to move away from here.'

'You think there'll be another earthquake?' asked Vana.

'That wasn't an earthquake, my dear.'

'Well, whatever it was, the noise was coming from the Machine. It seems to have stopped now.'

'Exactly,' said the Doctor. 'Which means that the Krotons have time to attend to us. Haven't you finished yet, Zoe?'

'No, I haven't. Can I borrow your braces, Doctor?'

'Certainly not,' said the Doctor clutching them protectively. He snatched the bandana handkerchief from his breast pocket and passed it to her. 'I'd much rather you used this!'

Zoe took the big handkerchief. 'That'll do.' She twisted it into a rope and used it to finish binding Thara's leg.

Selris came to join them. Sadly he surveyed the devastation around them. 'We have failed. The Machine is undamaged.'

'I wouldn't be too sure,' said the Doctor gently. 'Just take a look at it.'

Now that much of the Learning Hall had been

destroyed, the curved wall at the end could be seen as part of an enormous dome, on and around which the Learning Hall had been built.

A dull black stain was spreading patchily over the done's silvery surface.

'What's happening to it, Doctor?' asked Selris.

'I'm not sure, but I'd say it was no longer functioning under full power. Vana, how is Beta getting along with that acid I asked for?'

'I've just been back to see him, Doctor. He sent you this.' She produced the little phial. 'He only made a small amount to start with.'

The Doctor unstoppered the phial and sniffed at it gingerly.

'Is it all right?' asked Vana anxiously.

'Oh yes, I think so, my dear.'

Zoe took the phial and sniffed it. 'It's sulphuric acid!'

'Basically, with one or two extras added. Don't touch it, it burns!' The Doctor took back the phial, restoppered it and handed it back to Vana. 'Look after it for a moment — it's terribly important.'

Suddenly Zoe said, 'Doctor, what about Jamie? We came here to look for him, remember?'

'So we did,' said the Doctor guiltily. 'I'd forgotten with all this excitement.'

Zoe turned to Selris. 'Has anybody seen him?'

Selris hesitated. 'I thought you knew. He followed you into the Machine.'

'When?' demanded Zoe.

'I'm not really sure. It wasn't long after you and the Doctor went in.'

Zoe looked at the Doctor in horror. 'Jamie wouldn't be any use to them. His mind is completely untrained!'

The Doctor nodded. 'Yes, quite so. And if the

Machine rejected him like the others . . . come on, Zoe!'

Grabbing Zoe's hand, the Doctor almost dragged her up the steps.

By now Jamie had made his way through the noisy and chaotic corridors of the Kroton ship, negotiated the forest of dangling nutrient pipes and now found himself at a dead end — the antechamber before the closed back door.

The door was of course immoveable, and after several attempts to shift it, Jamie crouched down on his heels, very close to despair. Now that the crisis in the ship was over the Krotons would realise he'd gone and come looking for him.

Suddenly Jamie spotted a gleaming fragment of a stone at his feet. He picked it up. It was the Doctor's bit of mica.

Jamie's mind might have been untrained, but he was bright enough in his own way, especially where his own survival was at stake.

He picked up the piece of mica and studied it. It had been lying directly under that circular socket thing just to one side of the door. And if the Doctor had used it to get out . . .

Selris was directing the treatment of the wounded and the clearing up of the Learning Hall when Eelek marched down the steps, his henchman Axus at his side.

Behind them came the usual bodyguard of pikemen.

Eelek raised his voice so that all the Gonds in the hall could hear. 'Well, Selris, are you satisfied now?'

Axus had been checking on the extent of the disaster. 'There are seven of his working party unaccounted for. I think we have four more badly injured. Two of them are probably going to die.'

'The wounded are being cared for,' said Selris angrily. 'I have arranged —'

'No!' snapped Eelek. He gestured dramatically around the ruined hall. 'You have done enough already.'

'You were the one who wanted to fight the Krotons,' said Selris grimly.

Since this was undoubtedly true, Eelek was forced to take refuge in more politician's rhetoric. 'I will fight the Krotons in my own time and in my own way,' he announced grandly.

'My way is better,' insisted Selris. 'The Krotons are invulnerable inside their Machine, but if we can lure them out . . . '

Axus came to the support of his leader. 'You've had your chance, Selris, and look what you've achieved. The Learning Hall is ruined, our people are dead and wounded, and the Machine is untouched.'

Selris pointed to the spreading stain. 'The Machine has been *damaged*.'

Eelek seized his moment. 'Damaged?' he shouted. 'It must be *destroyed!* I intend to launch a mass attack with slings and fireballs. They are in position now.'

'And the Krotons will turn our city into another Wasteland.' Wearily Selris turned away. 'You're a fool, Eelek.'

'And you are a traitor!' screamed Eelek. 'See what your stupidity has done. You were dispaced as Leader of the Council. You had no authority to order this attack.'

'Leadership of the Council has long been hereditary. My son Thara will replace me.'

'No!' shouted Eelek. '*I* have replaced you. Guards, arrest him!'

The pikemen moved forward.

'Wait,' protested Selris. 'This is no time to be fighting amongst ourselves. At least let me help you organise the attack.'

'I don't need your help, Selris. You had your chance — and you failed.'

Selris wasn't listening. He was looking over Eelek's shoulder. 'Have I failed? Have I, Eelek?' Selris's voice was grim. 'I said I would bring the Krotons out of the Machine.'

Eelek whirled round.

A Kroton was standing in the open doorway of the Machine.

11

Eelek's Bargain

For a moment Eelek stared at the great silvery figure in awe. Here was one of the gods he had worshipped all his life, the master he had served faithfully for so many years.

He studied the massive silver body, the immense torso and high ridged shoulders, the clamp-like hands and the terrifying blank silver head rising to a point.

One of the hands had a huge bulbous device attached to it, clearly a weapon of some kind. And the weapon was covering their little group.

For a moment Eelek had an impulse to fall down and worship, but things had gone too far for that. Summoning all his courage, he stepped forward.

'Stop!' boomed the Kroton.

Eelek froze. Struggling to keep his voice steady he said, 'What do you want?'

'Where are the two high brains?'

'I don't understand —'

'The two alien creatures are needed urgently. Where are they?'

'He means the Doctor and Zoe,' said Selris quietly. He raised his voice. 'Why do you want them?'

'Unimportant!' boomed the Kroton. 'Produce them.'

Eelek was thinking hard. 'They're not here.'

'Where are they?'

Eelek was nothing if not a politician. He could smell the chance of a bargain, of making some kind of deal. 'You say you *need* them. Why are they so important to you? You've never come out of your Machine before.'

There was a young Gond standing watching events from halfway up the stairs. He wasn't a guard, wasn't even armed, just a too curious spectator.

Before anyone realised what was happening, the gaping muzzle of the Kroton's weapon swung round to cover him. There was a kind of hissing roar and the boy's body glowed brightly for a moment. He gave a single choked-off scream of agony — then he was gone.

'Why did you do that?' shouted Selris angrily. 'He wasn't harming you.'

It was all too clear why the Kroton had killed at random. It was a demonstration of ruthlessness and of power.

'Do not argue with us. You will produce the high brains in fifteen minutes.'

Despite the Kroton's terrifying demonstration, Eelek, courageous in his own way, was still pressing for some advantage. 'If we give you these strangers, will you leave us in peace?'

'The high brains will enable us to operate the drive mechanism of our ship.'

'Drive mechanism? You mean you'll go? You'll actually leave our world?'

'Yes. But if the two high brains are not brought to the Dynotrope you will all be dispersed. Do you understand?'

Eelek's voice was loud and confident, the voice of a leader. 'Very well. If you will promise to leave our world — you shall have them.'

The Kroton turned away and glided back into the ship.

'Why are you doing this?' asked Selris in anguish. 'Only a few hours ago you wanted to fight the Krotons.'

'I wanted to be rid of them,' corrected Eelek coldly. 'Why fight if we can get what we want without bloodshed? You heard what the Kroton said.'

'But the Doctor and Zoe are our friends. They risked their lives for our sakes.'

'I put the interests of our people first.' Eelek looked thoughtfully at Selris, Thara and Vana. All three were friendly towards the aliens. They would warn them if they got the chance.

'Axus, put these people under guard. I'll organise the search for the two aliens.'

Leaving Axus and a couple of pikemen behind, Eelek strode up the stairs.

Jamie was still fiddling irritatedly with the chunk of mica, trying to jam it into the socket and trip the door opening circuit.

He was just about to give up in despair when suddenly he succeeded — at least partially.

The door began to rise — then it jammed, leaving only a narrow gap between door and floor.

Jamie looked at it ruefully. It was a *very* narrow gap. But there was no alternative.

Flattening himself on the floor, Jamie wriggled forwards, trying to squeeze his brawny form through the little space. His head went through all right and then his shoulders, but somewhere around the waist area he stuck fast.

He wriggled furiously. Wasn't there some saying about where your head would go the rest would go — or was that only cats?

Jamie was still thrashing about on the ground like a stranded fish when the Doctor and Zoe came running across the Wasteland towards him.

'Look out, Jamie!' yelled the Doctor. 'Remember the poison spray!'

'Help me!' roared Jamie. 'This door's jammed, I can't move it!'

The Doctor and Zoe came panting up. The Doctor surveyed the struggling Jamie thoughtfully. 'Jammed, eh? That means the power is failing or — yes, that's it! The Krotons must have cut their auxiliary power motors.'

'Never mind all that, Doctor. Help me out!' bellowed Jamie.

'Oh dear, can't you get out? You're getting fat, Jamie. Come on, Zoe, lend a hand.'

They each grabbed an arm and started pulling. Jamie wriggled even more furiously than before and suddenly shot out of the gap like a cork from a bottle.

'Watch out!' yelled the Doctor. All three hurled themselves sideways off the ramp, just as the spray jets opened up.

The corrosive spray was less powerful this time, and by the time it was over the Doctor, Jamie and Zoe were sheltering under a nearby rock.

'What's been happening?' demanded Jamie. 'I thought yon machine was going to shake itself to pieces!'

'No time to explain,' said the Doctor, not for the first time. 'How are you feeling, Jamie?'

'Well —' began Jamie dubiously, about to launch on an account of his ordeal.

'Good,' said the Doctor briskly. 'Now Jamie, I want you to do something very important for me!'

'Not again,' groaned Jamie wearily.

'When we get back to the Gond city I want you to

104

go to Beta's laboratory. He's producing a special kind of sulphuric acid for me. I want you to tell him to make it in bulk — as much as he can manage — and bring it to the Learning Hall.'

'Aye, but —'

'No time to argue, Jamie. Hurry. When you've finished at Beta's you'll find us in the Learning Hall.'

A Gond sentry came hurrying into the Learning Hall and whispered a message to Eelek.

Eelek smiled and turned to one of his followers. 'The strangers are returning. You two, over there, you with me!'

Thara, Selris and Vana looked on helplessly as the two groups hid in the shadows on either side of the stairs.

'They're going to walk right into a trap,' whispered Vana.

'And Eelek talks about caring for the people,' muttered Selris disgustedly. 'All that really concerns him is power — and his own skin!'

Vana said softly. 'If we could warn the Doctor and the girl, perhaps they could escape in their own space machine.'

Selris nodded. 'Yes, we owe him that at least — a chance to escape . . . '

Faced with the Doctor's orders to make the acid in bulk, Beta simply rigged up a larger version of the apparatus that had produced the first phial.

The lash-up of beakers, burners and tubes was hissing and seething and bubbling on his main bench now, supervised by Jamie and himself.

Both wore cloths about their mouths to protect them from the choking fumes, and neither had very much idea of what they were actually doing.

They were having a series of rather muffled conversations.

'How long will it take?' asked Jamie.

'No idea,' said Beta cheerfully.

There was a hiss of steam and the whole lash-up shook alarmingly. Jamie backed away. 'It's no' going to explode, is it?'

'I don't know!'

'I thought you were supposed to be the scientist?'

'I am, but I've never worked with acids before. The Krotons always used to forbid it.'

He picked up a chunk of sulphurous rock and approached the bubbling cauldron.

'Shall I put in a bit more to speed things up?'

'Why ask me?'

'Let's see what happens,' said Beta philosophically. 'After all, we can only blow ourselves up.'

Beta, thought Jamie, was a scientist after the Doctor's own heart.

Beta tossed the chunk of rock into the cauldron, like a housewife adding another onion to the soup. The cauldron bubbled even more fiercely and a jet of sulphurous smoke spurted out of the apparatus.

Beta turned to Jamie. 'Do you think that was enough?'

'Well it was enough for me!' shouted Jamie above the din. 'Quite enough.'

His words were obliterated by another explosion, and another cloud of smoke.

'Selris, listen,' whispered Vana. 'You try to distract Axus while I slip up the stairs.'

'There are more men posted outside . . .'

'I might be able to get by them. Anyway, it's worth trying.'

Selris nodded. 'I agree. There's just a chance.' He

rose and moved over towards Axus, who had been watching the little group suspiciously. 'Axus, listen to me!'

'Well, what is it?'

Selris moved closer so that his bulk loomed over the smaller man, cutting off his view of Vana. 'In the past you've always accepted my judgement, Axus. Believe me, Eelek's wrong. It's a mistake to trust the Krotons.'

'I don't trust them. And Eelek's right. We're doing the only thing we can.'

From the corner of his eye, Selris could see Vana stealing towards the stairs. He edged round, using himself as a human screen, and leaned urgently towards Axus. 'If we surrender the strangers, the Krotons will kill us for certain.'

Axus stared at him. 'Why do you say that?'

'Of course they will. We mean nothing to them, we never have. But while we've still got the Doctor and Zoe we've got something to negotiate with!'

'But if we don't hand over the strangers the Krotons will kill us all for certain,' pointed out Axus triumphantly. 'You're growing old, Selris, your arguments make no sense.'

He moved clear of Selris — and suddenly realised that Vana was missing. Axus whirled round, just in time to see her vanishing up the stairs. 'Stop her! Stop that girl!'

Vana sprinted up the stairs and ran straight into two more guards. She tried to yell a warning just in case the Doctor was near. 'Doctor! Look —'

A hand was clamped over her mouth. The guards grabbed her and carried her, still struggling, to where Selris waited by the disabled Thara.

In the struggle, the stone phial was knocked from Vana's hand and rolled to Selris's feet. Automatically, he picked it up . . .

The Krotons were making final calculations.

'Balance zero plus twelve,' reported Kroton Two.

The Kroton Commander said, 'We have reserve power for twenty-seven minutes.'

'Then we shall exhaust.'

For once there was a hint of emotion, a tinge of sadness in the Kroton Commander's voice. 'Yes. Our function will end.'

The Doctor and Zoe were hurrying down the steps that led into the Learning Hall. They noticed quite a few armed Gonds about, but no-one made any attempt to stop them.

As they reached the bottom of the steps Zoe was saying, 'But what are we going to do, Doctor?'

'To be honest, Zoe, I'm not quite sure. I wish there was some way of getting into that machine —'

The Doctor broke off as Eelek appeared from the shadows.

'Oh, but there is, Doctor.' He gave them one of his peculiarly sinister smiles. 'We'll help you inside.'

'That's very kind of you,' began the Doctor. 'Wait a moment — what's all this?'

At a gesture from Eelek, Zoe and the Doctor were suddenly surrounded by armed guards. The Doctor glared indignantly at them. 'Now then, what are you doing? Look here . . . ' They were herded towards the Machine.

The Kroton Commander studied the scene on the monitor.

'The high brains have been captured. Balance check?'

'Zero plus nine.'

'Exhaust time, twenty-two minutes.'

'Shall I open the Dynotrope, Commander?'

'Yes. But only the two high brains must enter.'

'Take them up to the doors,' ordered Eelek.

'We won't be bullied, you know,' said the Doctor fiercely. 'Don't push!'

But despite the Doctor's protests, he and Zoe were half-shoved, half-dragged to the foot of the ramp.

The Doctor caught a glimpse of Vana hovering in the background. 'Vana!' he called. 'Have you got that phial?'

Vana suddenly realised that she hadn't — and that she had no idea where it was. She spread her hands helplessly.

'But I must have it,' called the Doctor. 'It's vital!'

The amplified Kroton voice boomed from the ship. 'THE HIGH BRAINS WILL ENTER IMMEDIATELY.'

The Gond guards levelled their pikes.

'We'd better do as they say Doctor,' said Zoe nervously.

'Yes, I suppose we had. Well, Zoe, ladies first — after you!'

The Doctor was still signalling frantically to Vana but it was already too late.

Zoe and the Doctor started up the ramp and the door began sliding upwards to admit them.

'The high brains are about to enter the Dynotrope, Commander,' reported Kroton Two.

'Prepare for take-off. Initiate Phase One.'

'Phase One ready. Shall I destroy the Gonds now? They are no longer of any value.'

The Commander considered. 'No. The dispersion units use power. We have no power to waste.'

Vana came hurrying up to Selris, who was watching events with an expression of grim helplessness.

'That bottle, Selris, with the liquid Beta made for the Doctor.'

Selris reached inside his tunic and produced the phial. 'It's all right, Vana. I have it safe — here.'

'The Doctor needs it — he says it's vital.'

By now the Doctor and Zoe had passed through the open door of the Kroton Machine and the door had started to descend.

Suddenly Selris began running towards the Machine. Thrusting the astonished guards aside he reached the top of the ramp just in time to throw himself down and roll under the door.

It closed behind him.

Once again the Doctor and Zoe found themselves in the Kroton control room. The Krotons were at their console and the Doctor noticed that both were already plugged into the central nutrient tank.

The Doctor drew himself up to his not-very-considerable height and confronted the two silver giants. 'I gather you wanted to speak with us?'

'You will now assist us with take-off.'

Suddenly Selris burst into the control room. 'Doctor!' he cried.

Selris had just time to hand the Doctor the phial — and then Kroton Two raised its weapon.

'No!' shouted the Doctor.

Selris leaped for the door but it was too late. It had closed behind him.

For a second his body glowed in the laser beam, the Doctor and Zoe heard a bellow of pain — and then Selris was gone.

Zoe buried her head on the Doctor's shoulder. The Doctor patted her back, thinking that Selris had not

sacrificed himself in vain. The phial was securely
clasped in the Doctor's other hand.

12

Acid

For the Krotons it seemed, the incident was already over. Thankfully the Doctor realised that their indifference to the motives of lesser beings made it unlikely they would even wonder why Selris had sacrificed his life.

It was a mistake, which the Doctor very much hoped would prove fatal. The Krotons' total egotistical callousness, he decided, made them one of the least attractive life forms he had ever encountered.

'Set up the intergalactic link,' ordered the Commander.

A strange device rose smoothly from the control room floor, a sort of four-sided console surmounted by a huge glowing coil.

Two headsets were linked to the console.

'Take-off, Phase Two,' said the Kroton Two.

'Prepare for take-off!'

'All systems set.'

The Commander turned to the Doctor. 'You will assist us now.'

'Assist you? In what way?'

'The Dynotrope will exhaust in twelve minutes.'

'That's your problem,' muttered Zoe rebelliously.

'Not entirely, Zoe,' said the Doctor quietly. 'If this

machine runs down there will be a colossal energy release. Enough to destroy us, the Krotons, the Gonds and maybe the entire planet.' He turned back to the Krotons. 'You'll have to explain what you want us to do.' He pointed to the four-side console. 'What's this thing?'

'It is the intergalactic link. It transfers the Dynotrope to our own cosmos. It operates through mental power.'

'You've really discovered a way of transforming mental power into energy?' Even the Doctor was impressed. It had long been known that mental power was the greatest energy source in the cosmos — in a sense, it *was* the cosmos — but no-one as yet had discovered an effective way of tapping it. No wonder these Krotons had such a high opinion of themselves.

Zoe, however, wasn't so impressed. 'And you Krotons haven't enough mental power of your own to make it work?'

'Four high brains are needed in relay. There are only two of us.'

'Then how did you get it here?'

'No more questions.'

'If you want our co-operation, you must expect questions,' said the Doctor.

Kroton Two raised its weapon. 'Unless you do as we order you will be dispersed.'

'Maybe so,' said the Doctor cheerfully. 'But that won't help you much, will it?'

The Commander, it seemed, was prepared to make concessions. 'We are wasting time. The Dynotrope was part of a battle fleet. The other two members of the crew were exhausted by enemy fire.'

'You mean they were killed?' asked Zoe.

The Kroton answered in its own strange terminology. 'They exhausted. They ceased to function. We

114

carried out emergency procedure and landed on the nearest planet. To conserve power, we set the Dyno-trope in perpetual stability.'

'I see,' said the Doctor intrigued. 'Then you set up the Teaching Machines to educate the natives up to the mental standards you require.'

'That is so. They were primitives.'

'You still didn't have to kill them!'

'Gond samples were brought in for testing at regular intervals. The Dynotrope absorbed their mental power into its circuits. The waste matter was ejected and dispersed.'

Before the angry Doctor could speak the second Kroton turned from its study of the console. 'Nine minutes to exhaust time, Commander.'

Jamie and Beta staggered into the Learning Hall carrying an enormous glass jar between them. Liquid sloshed about inside and acrid fumes seeped through the cloth stretched over the jar's mouth.

Axus marched officiously up to them. 'Where do you think you're going? What's that?'

'It's something called acid,' said Beta with dignity. 'The Doctor asked me to make it for him.'

Axus laughed. 'He'll have no need of it now. You've been wasting your time, Beta.'

'Where is he?' demanded Jamie.

'He has joined the Krotons.'

Beta gaped at him. 'In the Machine?'

'That's right.'

'And what about Zoe?' asked Jamie.

Vana came hurrying up to them. 'Zoe too. The Krotons wanted them — and Eelek surrendered them.'

'He did *what?*'

Eelek came by just in time to hear his name

mentioned. 'The Krotons needed your friends in order to be able to leave our world,' he explained calmly.

'And you just handed them over, did you?' asked Jamie menacingly.

'If the Krotons will leave our world, they are welcome to your friends.'

Jamie drew back his fist. 'Why you miserable —'

Armed guards moved forward, and Beta put a restraining hand on Jamie's shoulder. 'Careful, Jamie.'

Eelek turned contemptuously away. 'It's time we were all leaving.'

'Leaving?' said Jamie indignantly.

Eelek paused on the stairs. 'Unless you all want to die.'

Beta gave him a puzzled look. 'What are you talking about Eelek?'

Eelek sighed. 'For a scientist, Beta, you are very stupid. This Learning Hall, and for all we know most of our City is built around the Krotons' Machine. And if that Machine goes back into the sky . . . '

Beta blenched. 'This whole place will come down.'

'Exactly. Do you really want to be buried alive?'

'Well, I'm staying,' said Jamie doggedly. 'I'm getting the Doctor and Zoe out of there somehow. Beta?'

'All right. I'll stay and help you, Jamie.'

Eelek looked at Vana. 'And you, Vana?'

'I'm staying to look after Thara. Unlike you, Eelek, I'm not sensible enough to run away and leave my friends.'

Eelek's face was impassive. After a moment he said calmly. 'Very well. Let them stay — and let them die.' Eelek and his men disappeared up the stairs.

Beta gave Jamie a rueful look. 'He could be right, you know.'

'Aye, mebbe,' said Jamie philosophically. 'But at least we can put up a fight.' He tapped the smoking jar. 'Now then, where are we going to put this stuff?'

Beta smiled. 'I know the very place.'

The Doctor and the Krotons were approaching their final confrontation.

The Doctor had delayed with questions and objections as long as he dared, but now the Commander was losing patience. 'Put on the head-sets.'

'Just one more thing,' said the Doctor. 'If you transfer the Dynotrope back to your own world — what will happen to us?'

'You will suffer no harm.'

'How can we be sure you're telling the truth?' argued the Doctor. 'You see, we should die without oxygen — *just as you would die if anything upset the nutrient supply you draw from that tank.*'

The Doctor gave Zoe a nudge — and passed her the stone phial behind both their backs.

Moving forward, he attempted to distract the Krotons while Zoe edged backwards towards the tank, the phial held behind her.

'Take up your positions,' ordered the Commander.

'All right, all right,' said the Doctor. 'I'm only telling Zoe that if, by any chance, something contaminated the contents of that tank, you'd know what it was like to breathe poisoned air.'

'Six minutes to exhaust time,' reported Kroton Two.

The Commander was becoming angry and suspicious. 'You have no choice. Put the head-set on now.'

By now Zoe was standing with her back against the side of the tank. She unstoppered the phial, being very careful to hold it upright, and then swiftly tipped its entire contents into the tank. She looked up, caught the Doctor's eye and nodded briefly.

The Doctor addressed the Kroton. 'Oh well, I suppose we'll have to take your word.' He moved across to the console.

'Set the transfer link,' ordered the Commander.

'Final phase on automatic.'

'Now then,' said the Doctor fussily. 'Where do you want me to stand?'

'Unimportant.'

'Oh, very well. I'll stand over here then.' The Doctor moved to the nearest place at the console. He gave Zoe a meaningful look.

'Oh, *I* wanted to stand there,' she protested.

'My dear Zoe,' said the Doctor. 'In that case, you must stand here, and I'll stand over there.'

In this way they managed to waste several minutes.

'Put on the head-sets at once or you will be dispersed,' ordered the Commander.

The Doctor seemed to be thoroughly confused. 'We're doing our best. Now, which way do they go? This way? No, this way!'

Zoe glanced at the tank. 'Nothing seems to be happening,' she whispered.

'No,' said the Doctor grimly. 'Perhaps in a minute . . . Play for time.' He fumbled with his head-set and managed to drop it. 'Oops! Butterfingers!'

It seemed insane to be clowning at a time of such danger, but Zoe made herself join in. 'Oh, you are clumsy, Doctor!'

'Enough of this!' boomed the Commander. 'Put on the head-sets or you will be dispersed.'

'It's all your fault,' babbled the Doctor. 'You're making me nervous.' He put on his head-set as slowly as he dared.

Zoe did the same, and winced as she felt a sudden tug at her mind. She felt locked in, a part of the

Machine. Had the Krotons won after all?

Suddenly the Commander made a ghastly gurgling sound, staggered back from the console, and crashed to the ground.

Kroton Two tottered back, weaving to and fro, trying to bring its weapon to bear on the Doctor and Zoe. It managed a few words of slurred and gurgling speech: 'What — what have you . . . '

'Down, Zoe!' yelled the Doctor. They threw themselves to one side as the Kroton toppled over backwards like a falling tree. The laser cannon blazed harmlessly at the ceiling.

The Doctor helped Zoe to her feet. 'Are you all right?'

Zoe was staring down at the fallen Krotons. 'Look at them,' she whispered. 'They're — *dissolving!*'

The massive silver bodies were crumbling away before their eyes, collapsing into a kind of shapeless sludge that dribbled away from the decaying figures.

'Yes, they're returning to their basic forms . . . '

Zoe coughed. 'Doctor, these fumes. They're choking . . . '

'I know. We've got to get out of here.' He looked round and then pointed. 'Look, Zoe, the Machine's melting too!'

Great chunks of wall were sliding away, as the Machine mirrored the disintegration of its Kroton masters. The Doctor grabbed Zoe's arm. 'Let's get out of here before we're trapped!'

They hurried through the distorted, dissolving corridors and found the main door already half-eaten away.

A few vigorous kicks from the Doctor disposed of the rest of it and they emerged into the ruins of the Learning Hall.

The place seemed empty . . .

Suddenly they heard voices, shouts and a great deal of coughing coming from below.

They ran down the stairs that led to the Underhall. There they found Beta and Jamie, both with cloths tied over their mouths, pouring the remains of a huge pot of acid into the pit that had been dug by the main pillar.

The Doctor rapped Jamie on the shoulder. 'Hello!' he said, cheerfully.

Jamie turned round. 'Doctor! Zoe!'

Beta looked up. 'What's happening?'

Jamie couldn't believe his eyes. 'Are you all right, both of you? Are you hurt?'

'Just a little shaken, Jamie. But believe me we're much better off than the Krotons!'

In the corner of the Learning Hall, Thara was being nursed by Vana. Suddenly he pointed, 'Look, Vana. Look at the Machine!'

By now the whole dome was disintegrating, caving into nothingness. 'It's working, Thara,' said Vana joyfully. 'Look, it's working!'

Jamie, Zoe, Beta and the Doctor came hurrying up the stairs to join them.

'What made you think of pouring acid on the Machine?' asked Zoe.

Beta laughed. 'We reckoned if the Doctor thought a few drops were so important, we'd see what a few gallons would do!'

Zoe turned to the Doctor. 'And how did you know that the Krotons and the Machine would dissolve, Doctor?'

'Mmm? Well, the Machine was about eighty per cent tellurium, you know, and tellurium is soluble in sulphuric acid.'

'But the Machine wasn't pure tellurium . . . '

'Well, the acid wasn't pure sulphuric acid,' said the

Doctor cheerfully. 'Anyway, it worked, didn't it?'

Beta and Vana and Thara were all talking excitedly.

The Doctor nudged Jamie and Zoe. 'Come on you two, I hate goodbyes.' They slipped quietly up the stairs.

'Well, it's finished now isn't it?' Vana was saying.

'Yes, it's finished,' said Thara. 'The end of the Krotons. We're free at last.'

Beta frowned. 'There's still Eelek to deal with.'

Thara smiled grimly. 'That will be my pleasure. I shall succeed my father as leader of the Council — *whatever* Eelek thinks.'

'And now we can develop our own sciences,' said Beta eagerly. 'The Doctor will help us.' He looked round. 'Doctor?'

'They've gone,' said Thara gently.

'But I wanted to ask his advice,' protested Beta.

Thara smiled. 'There are no Krotons now, no Doctor. We shall have to find our own answers, Beta. Just us!'

In the Wasteland only the dying echoes of a faint wheezing, groaning sound remained to show that the Doctor and his companions were on their way to new adventures.

DOCTOR WHO

	TERRANCE DICKS **Doctor Who and The**	
0426114558	**Abominable Snowmen**	£1.35
0426200373	**Doctor Who and The** **Android Invasion**	£1.25
0426201086	**Doctor Who and The** **Androids of Tara**	£1.35
0426116313	IAN MARTER **Doctor Who and The** **Ark in Space**	£1.35
0426201043	TERRANCE DICKS **Doctor Who and The** **Armageddon Factor**	£1.50
0426112954	**Doctor Who and The** **Auton Invasion**	£1.50
0426116747	**Doctor Who and The** **Brain of Morbius**	£1.35
0426110250	**Doctor Who and The** **Carnival of Monsters**	£1.35
042611471X	MALCOLM HULKE **Doctor Who and** **The Cave Monsters**	£1.50
0426117034	TERRANCE DICKS **Doctor Who and The** **Claws of Axos**	£1.35
042620123X	DAVID FISHER **Doctor Who and The** **Creature from the Pit**	£1.35
0426113160	DAVID WHITAKER **Doctor Who and The Crusaders**	£1.50
0426200616	BRIAN HAYLES **Doctor Who and The Curse** **of Peladon**	£1.50
0426114639	GERRY DAVIS **Doctor Who and The Cybermen**	£1.50
0426113322	BARRY LETTS **Doctor Who and The Daemons**	£1.50

Prices are subject to alteration

DOCTOR WHO

	DAVID WHITAKER	
0426101103	**Doctor Who and The Daleks**	£1.50
042611244X	**TERRANCE DICKS** **Doctor Who and The Dalek Invasion of Earth**	£1.50
0426103807	**Doctor Who and The Day of the Daleks**	£1.35
042620042X	**Doctor Who – Death to the Daleks**	£1.35
0426119657	**Doctor Who and The Deadly Assassin**	£1.50
0426200969	**Doctor Who and The Destiny of the Daleks**	£1.35
0426108744	**MALCOLM HULKE** **Doctor Who and The Dinosaur Invasion**	£1.35
0426103726	**Doctor Who and The Doomsday Weapon**	£1.50
0426201464	**IAN MARTER** **Doctor Who and The Enemy of the World**	£1.50
0426200063	**TERRANCE DICKS** **Doctor Who and The Face of Evil**	£1.50
0426201507	**ANDREW SMITH** **Doctor Who – Full Circle**	£1.50
0426112601	**TERRANCE DICKS** **Doctor Who and The Genesis of the Daleks**	£1.35
0426112792	**Doctor Who and The Giant Robot**	£1.35
0426115430	**MALCOLM HULKE** **Doctor Who and The Green Death**	£1.35

Prices are subject to alteration

DOCTOR WHO

	TERRANCE DICKS **Doctor Who and The** **Hand of Fear**	
0426200330		£1.35
	Doctor Who and The **Horns of Nimon**	
0426201310		£1.35
	Doctor Who and The **Horror of Fang Rock**	
0426200098		£1.35
	BRIAN HAYLES **Doctor Who and The** **Ice Warriors**	
0426108663		£1.35
	Doctor Who and The **Image of the Fendahl**	
0426200772		£1.35
	TERRANCE DICKS **Doctor Who and The** **Invasion of Time**	
0426200934		£1.35
	Doctor Who and The **Invisible Enemy**	
0426200543		£1.35
	Doctor Who and The **Keeper of Traken**	
0426201485		£1.35
	PHILIP HINCHCLIFFE **Doctor Who and The** **Keys of Marinus**	
0426201256		£1.35
	DAVID FISHER **Doctor Who and The** **Leisure Hive**	
0426201477		£1.35
	TERRANCE DICKS **Doctor Who and The** **Loch Ness Monster**	
0426110412		£1.25
	CHRISTOPHER H BIDMEAD **Doctor Who – Logopolis**	
0426201493		£1.35
	PHILIP HINCHCLIFFE **Doctor Who and The** **Masque of Mandragora**	
0426118936		£1.25
	TERRANCE DICKS **Doctor Who and The** **Monster of Peladon**	
0426201329		£1.35

Prices are subject to alteration

DOCTOR WHO

0426116909	Doctor Who and The Mutants	£1.35
0426201302	Doctor Who and The Nightmare of Eden	£1.35
0426112520	Doctor Who and The Planet of the Daleks	£1.35
0426116828	Doctor Who and The Planet of Evil	£1.35
0426106555	Doctor Who and The Planet of the Spiders	£1.35
0426201019	Doctor Who and The Power of Kroll	£1.50
0426116666	Doctor Who and The Pyramids of Mars	£1.35
042610997X	Doctor Who and The Revenge of the Cybermen	£1.35
0426200926	IAN MARTER Doctor Who and The Ribos Operation	£1.50
0426200616	TERRANCE DICKS Doctor Who and The Robots of Death	£1.35
042611308X	MALCOLM HULKE Doctor Who and The Sea Devils	£1.35
0426116586	PHILIP HINCHCLIFFE Doctor Who and The Seeds of Doom	£1.35
0426200497	IAN MARTER Doctor Who and The Sontaran Experiment	£1.35
0426110331	MALCOLM HULKE Doctor Who and The Space War	£1.35
0426201337	TERRANCE DICKS Doctor Who and The State of Decay	£1.35

Prices are subject to alteration

DOCTOR WHO

	0426200993	**Doctor Who and The Stones of Blood**	£1.35
	0426200594	**Doctor Who and The Sunmakers**	£1.50
☐	0426119738	**Doctor Who and The Talons of Weng Chiang**	£1.35
	0426110684	GERRY DAVIS **Doctor Who and The Tenth Planet**	£1.35
	0426115007	TERRANCE DICKS **Doctor Who and The Terror of the Autons**	£1.35
	0426115783	**Doctor Who – The Three Doctors**	£1.50
	0426200233	**Doctor Who and The Time Warriors**	£1.50
	0426110765	GERRY DAVIS **Doctor Who and The Tomb of the Cybermen**	£1.35
	0426200683	TERRANCE DICKS **Doctor Who and The Underworld**	£1.35
	0426201442	**Doctor Who and An Unearthly Child**	£1.35
	0426201353	ERIC SAWARD **Doctor Who and The Visitation**	£1.35
	0426200829	MALCOLM HULKE **Doctor Who and The War Games**	£1.50
	0426201469	JOHN LYDECKER **Doctor Who and Warriors' Gate**	£1.35
	0426110846	TERRANCE DICKS **Doctor Who and The Web of Fear**	£1.35
	0426113241	BILL STRUTTON **Doctor Who and The Zarbi**	£1.50

Prices are subject to alteration

DOCTOR WHO

ISBN		Price
0426192974	PETER GRIMWADE **Doctor Who – Time-Flight**	£1.50
0426201361	TERRANCE DICKS **Doctor Who – Meglos**	£1.35
0426193261	CHRISTOPHER H. BIDMEAD **Doctor Who – Castrovalva**	£1.50
0426193342	TERRANCE DICKS **Doctor Who – Four to Doomsday**	£1.35
0426193776	IAN MARTER **Doctor Who – Earthshock**	£1.35
0426193857	JOHN LYDECKER **Doctor Who – Terminus**	£1.50
0426193423	TERRANCE DICKS **Doctor Who – Arc of Infinity**	£1.35
0426195108	**Doctor Who – The Five Doctors**	£1.50
0426193938	PETER GRIMWADE **Doctor Who – Mawdryn Undead**	£1.35
0426194578	TERRANCE DICKS **Doctor Who – Snakedance**	£1.35
0426195299	**Doctor Who – Kinda**	£1.35
042619537X	BARBARA CLEGG **Doctor Who – Enlightenment**	£1.50
0426195531	IAN MARTER **Doctor Who – The Dominators**	£1.50
0426195612	TERRANCE DICKS **Doctor Who – Warriors of the Deep**	£1.50
0426195884	JOHN LUCAROTTI **Doctor Who – The Aztecs**	£1.50
0426196171	TERRANCE DICKS **Doctor Who – Inferno**	£1.50
0426196767	GERRY DAVIS **Doctor Who – The Highlanders**	£1.50
0426197801	CHRISTOPHER H. BIDMEAD **Doctor Who – Frontios**	£1.50

Prices are subject to alteration

THIS OFFER EXCLUSIVE TO

READERS

Pin up magnificent full colour posters of DOCTOR WHO

Just send £2.50 for the first poster and £1.25 for each additional poster

TO: PUBLICITY DEPARTMENT
W. H. ALLEN & CO PLC
44 HILL STREET
LONDON W1X 8LB

Cheques, Postal Orders made payable to WH Allen PLC

POSTER 1 ☐	**POSTER 2** ☐	**POSTER 3** ☐
POSTER 4 ☐	**POSTER 5** ☐	

Please allow 28 DAYS for delivery.

I enclose £ _____

CHEQUE NO. _____

ACCESS, VISA CARD NO. _____

Name _____

Address _____

_____